A king's life wasn't his—he knew that all too well. His own needs, his own desires, his own likes would always be second to duty.

And Idris saw his duty all too clearly. All of it.

His mind raced as he ruthlessly ousted all emotions from his mind, concentrating on the cold, hard facts, looking for the path ahead. First, it was clearly in the baby's best interests to have a mother's care right from birth. Secondly, he—Idris—was the legal heir, whether he liked it or not. But, thirdly, at the same time the unborn baby was the rightful heir. Fourthly, he was said baby's guardian.

The pieces began to fall into place one by one.

What had the lawyer said? That if a man was married to the mother when a child was born then he was automatically that child's legal father, regardless of actual paternity?

He looked over at the other man. 'Let me get this straight. If I marry *Sayeda* Saskia then the baby will be my child, my heir, both in law and in the eyes of the world?'

The lawyer's answer was drowned out by Saskia's indignant voice.

'There is no way I would marry you, Idris Delacour, not if you were the

But Idris saw the la d
to do. For Fayaz, fo

He had to marry Sa

Dear Reader,

It's been a cold, wet and grey winter here in Yorkshire, so it's been a real pleasure to spend the last few months in the fictional Middle Eastern country of Dalmaya. The beauty of creating my own country is that I'm not bound by pesky real-life geographical impossibilities; if I want Dalmaya to have a long coastline, rolling sand dunes punctuated by green oases and impenetrable mountains, then it absolutely can. And my hours of staring at beautiful mosaics, hammocks overlooking the sea and infinity pools completely counts as research!

Dalmaya might be a beautiful—and warm!—country, but neither Idris nor Saskia ever intended to make their home there. Saskia is living there temporarily, after agreeing to be a surrogate for an old friend. Meanwhile, much as Idris loves his mother's country, he's never felt he truly belongs there.

When a terrible accident propels Idris to the throne with Saskia by his side, the two of them realise that their own wishes and feelings come second to doing what's right—but there's a long and painful history between the pair. Can they overcome that history? Or are they doomed to make the same mistakes all over again?

I loved being whisked away to Dalmaya—I hope you love it too.

Love,

Jessica x

THE SHEIKH'S PREGNANT BRIDE

BY

JESSICA GILMORE

First Published in Great Britain 2017
By Mills & Boon, an imprint of HarperCollins*Publishers*
1 London Bridge Street, London, SE1 9GF

ISBN: 978-0-263-06992-1

Our policy is to use papers that are natural, renewable and recyclable products and made from wood grown in sustainable forests. The logging and manufacturing processes conform to the legal environmental regulations of the country of origin.

Printed and bound in Great Britain
by CPI Antony Rowe, Chippenham, Wiltshire

A former au pair, bookseller, marketing manager and seafront trader, **Jessica Gilmore** now works for an environmental charity in York, England. Married with one daughter, one fluffy dog and two dog-loathing cats, she spends her time avoiding housework and can usually be found with her nose in a book. Jessica writes emotional romance with a hint of humour, a splash of sunshine and a great deal of delicious food—and equally delicious heroes!

Books by Jessica Gilmore

Mills & Boon Romance

Summer at Villa Rosa

A Proposal from the Crown Prince

Maids Under the Mistletoe

Her New Year Baby Secret

The Life Swap

Unveiling the Bridesmaid
In the Boss's Castle

Summer Weddings

Expecting the Earl's Baby

His Reluctant Cinderella
The Heiress's Secret Baby
A Will, a Wish...a Proposal
Proposal at the Winter Ball

Visit the Author Profile page
at millsandboon.co.uk for more titles.

To Rufus.

All these years I thought I was a cat person—
turns out I'm all about the canine. Thank you for
letting me talk plots through at you, for all those
head-clearing walks and for keeping me company
through long hours at my keyboard. xxx

CHAPTER ONE

He'd said he'd be there in twelve hours, but in the end it was barely eight hours after he'd received the earth-shattering phone call when Idris Delacour strode into the cool, dark Council Chamber, his eyes still shielded against the harsh sun that had greeted him at the airport despite the still early hour. Grimly he stood by the empty seat at the end of the long table and, taking off his sunglasses, regarded the four sombre men who had stood at his entrance. They were all dressed in the customary long white robes and headdresses worn by traditionalists in Dalmaya and Idris's dark trousers and grey shirt looked both drab and shockingly modern by contrast.

He nodded at the men and waited until they took their seats before seating himself in the ornately carved wooden chair. He was aware of every curve, every bump in the ancient seat. A seat that should never have been his. A seat he was all too willing to relinquish. He cleared his throat. *'Salam.'*

They repeated the greeting back to him, the words barely uttered before he continued, 'There can be no mistake?'

'None, Your Highness.'

He flinched at the title but there was more pressing

business than his own unwanted and tenuous claim to the Dalmayan throne. 'They are both dead?'

'The King and Her Majesty, yes.'

'Terrorism?' Idris already knew the answers. He had asked the same question during the shock call that had shaken the entire chateau just eight hours before and had been extensively briefed and updated both whilst travelling to the airport and again once on the private jet that had awaited him there.

'We'll have to investigate further obviously,' the grey-faced man to his right answered. Idris recognised him as Sheikh Ibrahim Al Kouri, Dalmaya's Head of Security. 'But it doesn't seem so. It looks like it was simply a tragic accident.'

Simply? Such an odd way to describe the annihilation of an entire family. The better half of Idris's own family. 'And what? The car simply ran off the road?'

The General shook his head. 'The King and his wife were returning from a day's excursion and I believe His Majesty may have challenged the guards in the accompanying car to a race.' He paused. 'It would not have been the first time.'

Of course not. Fayaz loved to compete, always wanting to prove he was a winner in his own right, not just because of the privilege of his birth.

Sheikh Ibrahim continued in the same monotone voice, shock seemed to have flattened all his usual military pomp. 'The road was flat and empty and should have been quite safe but it would seem that either His Majesty or the other driver lost control of the wheel and crashed into the other car with a loss of all lives. We have experts on the scene and should have more information for you imminently.' He looked down at his notes. 'Four of my agents were in the crash.'

Idris pinched the top of his nose, the words spinning around in his head. He could see the scene so clearly: Fayaz laughing as the open-topped four-wheel drives wove in and out of each other's path on the wide, sand-covered road, encouraged by the screams of Maya, his wife and Queen. At what point had those screams become real—or had it all been over too fast for any of the party to be aware of how the game would end? He hoped so. He hoped they were laughing right until the end; it would be how he remembered them. Happy and so full of life it hurt.

'I'm sorry. Please pass on my condolences to your agents' families and take care of any outstanding pension and compensation arrangements.'

The General nodded and Idris turned to the man on his left, Minister of the Interior and his own great-uncle. 'What happens next?'

Sheikh Malik Al Osman pushed his tablet to one side. His eyes were heavy, his shoulders slumped as if he couldn't bear the burden that had fallen upon him. 'We've kept news of the accident under wraps while we made sure of no hostile involvement, but now you're here we'll brief state media and Parliament. The funerals will take place this evening and the official mourning period will commence then.'

Idris nodded. 'And then?'

Sheikh Ibrahim jumped in. 'Your Majesty. You know the terms of your grandfather's will. His Highness Sheikh Fayaz Al Osman and his line inherited the throne of Dalmaya, but if he died without issue then the kingdom passes to you and your line.'

Of course Idris *knew* this. Technically he had always been aware he was Fayaz's legal heir. He remembered the shock—a shock mingled with the warmth of acceptance—when his grandfather's will had been made public, cementing him firmly into the family. But the prospect of actually *becoming* King had been so far away he had never considered he would actually be called to do so. Fayaz had already been married at the time of their grandfather's death and his wife was young and healthy. There was no reason to believe they wouldn't soon have many children of their own to take precedence over Idris.

Besides, despite his grandfather's decree, Idris knew how unorthodox his claim was. 'My claim to the throne is through my mother. No King has ever inherited through the maternal line before.' Not only that but his mother's name was a byword for scandal in Dalmaya and, possibly even more unconventionally, his father was French—would the people of this proud kingdom accept the son of such a pair as their ruler?

The point was moot. His vineyard, chateau and his wine export business were all the kingdom Idris needed. He was fond of Dalmaya but he had no intention of living and ruling there. He didn't belong.

'Your grandfather's will…' the General repeated, but from the corner of his eye Idris saw a speculative look pass over his great-uncle's face and turned back to him.

'What do you think, Sheikh Malik?' Hope twisted in his chest, mingling with the fatigue and grief already consuming him. He knew how hard his grandfather had worked to keep the kingdom safe, to modernise it, to introduce universal healthcare and education. He couldn't just walk away from that legacy, not if there was no other option. But the Al Osman family was extensive. Surely there must be someone qualified and near enough the ruling branch for Idris to be able to hand over the crown with a clear conscience?

His uncle looked directly at Idris. 'His Excellency is of course correct and if Fayaz died without any issue you are by law the next King. But there *is* the baby...'

Idris blinked. He'd seen Maya just a few months ago and she hadn't mentioned any pregnancy. Besides, Fayaz would have told him straight away if he had had a child. Wouldn't he? 'The baby?' The rest of the table looked as confused as he felt. 'What baby?'

Saskia stretched and stared out at the enticing view. The sky was so bright and blue it almost hurt, the colour mirrored in the infinity pool just outside the folding glass doors and in the still sea beyond that. Another beautiful day in paradise, and if she could just drag herself off the insanely comfortable sofa and brave the intense heat for the ten seconds it took to step outside the air-conditioned villa and plunge into the pool then she would definitely have a swim. After all, the pool was the only place she was truly comfortable any more, her weight buoyed by the water, her bulk less ungainly.

Her hands strayed down to the tight bump as she caressed it. Just six weeks to go. Not that she was exactly looking forward to what awaited her at the end of that six weeks despite her daily private pregnancy yoga lessons, her doula, personal midwife and the deluxe delivery suite already pre-booked and awaiting her arrival. Nothing but the best to ease the birth of the new Crown Prince or Princess of Dalmaya.

Stretching again, Saskia winced as her back twinged. Even with the best care possible, pregnancy was the most uncomfortable experience she had ever been through. *Don't be so spoiled*, she told herself firmly, heaving herself to her feet and padding towards the doors. She was safe, ultra-healthily fed, looked after and, more importantly, so was Jack. Once the baby was safely delivered and in the loving arms of his or her parents then she and her little brother could get back to their lives. Only this time she would be able to afford to give Jack the kind of childhood he deserved. And she would finally catch a break.

Right. Saskia heaved herself off the sofa and took an unsteady step and then another, regaining her balance as she did so. *Balance.* She missed that, along with being able to see her toes and not swiping things off tables with her belly when she turned around. A swim and then she would settle down and tackle the essay she had been putting off. She might have the money to go back to university thanks to Fayaz and Maya, but if she could just get the first year completed long distance then she would have more money for a house—and for Jack.

Shucking off the loose cotton robe she wore over the frankly vast maternity swimsuit, Saskia opened the door, almost recoiling from the scalding temperature that hit her the second she stepped out. She hurried as best she could to the pool and cautiously sat herself down by the side, near the wide steps that led down into its blissfully cool depths. Sitting on the floor without needing a forklift to help her back up, that was another simple pleasure she was looking forward to.

'Sorry, little one,' she murmured, her hand slipping back to her belly. 'I do appreciate what a good baby you've been to look after for Maya but I think we're both getting a little uncomfortable here. Besides, you must be looking forward to meeting your mummy and daddy, hmm? I know they can't wait to meet you.'

That was an understatement. Fayaz and Maya were determined to be there for every step of the pregnancy. They had recorded stories for Saskia to play for the baby daily so that their voices would be instantly familiar when it was born and Maya had been as regular a visitor as she could manage. 'Not long now,' Saskia continued as she slid her aching legs into the deliciously cool water. 'Mummy comes to live with us next week so she can spend every moment with you until she can take you home. Won't that be lovely?'

Sharing this huge, luxurious villa would be very different from the old days, gossiping in the college student kitchen, but Saskia was still looking forward to some heart-to-hearts with her old friend *and* to some adult company. Fayaz and Maya hadn't wanted anyone to know that Saskia was carrying their baby and so she had been confined to the villa since her arrival in Dalmaya nearly seven months ago. No matter how luxurious it might be, a place she wasn't allowed to leave couldn't help but feel like a prison. A self-imposed prison, sure; Saskia had known every single term and condition before she'd signed the surrogacy agreement, but a prison nonetheless.

She lowered herself into the water, a shiver of delight trembling through her as the cold enveloped her uncomfortably warm skin, and kicked off. She had been warned not to overexert herself and consciously made herself swim slow, considered lengths, concentrating on her breathing and the style of each stroke. Excited as she was to start her new life, there *were* some things about her prison she would miss. There were unlikely to be any infinity pools in her future, and in London grey skies were far more probable than this never-ending blue. Saskia turned onto her back and floated, eyes shut against the bright sun.

She didn't know how long she stayed there, an ungainly mermaid basking in the sunshine, but a prickling at her neck and a sense of unease penetrated through her sun-induced haze. Saskia opened her eyes slowly, lowering her body until she was treading water upright, her hair slicked back. Whatever, whoever it was that disturbed her was behind her, at the head of the pool. Slowly she turned, awareness of her vulnerability rippling through her. She stopped. Shock hitting her hard.

'Idris?'

It couldn't be. Maya had promised her he was in France and swore she would never reveal to him that Saskia had carried her baby. No one outside Maya and Fayaz's immediate family was supposed to know the baby had been born to a surrogate at all.

But of course Idris *was* their family.

Her toes found the bottom of the pool and Saskia anchored herself as she stared at the tall man regarding her inscrutably. He looked exactly the same as he had done seven years ago. No, there were a few small changes. He was more put together, less earnest than the young man she had once been so besotted with. It wasn't just the well-cut, if slightly crumpled suit, the expensively tousled haircut or the dark shadow grazing his cheeks and chin. It was the confidence in the way he carried himself, a self-assuredness that, for all his pretence, the younger Idris hadn't yet achieved. The harsh lines around his mouth were new and looked to be forged by fatigue and grief and the dark brown eyes were dull—at first anyway.

Saskia stood tall, wishing she weren't in a tight swimsuit and stuck in a swimming pool looking up at him like a suppliant, as recognition dawned and Idris's gaze kindled, his eyebrows snapping together.

'Saskia? What on earth are you doing here?' She'd forgotten the impact his voice had always had on her, low, almost gravelly, his French accent more of a hint than a full-on reminder of his heritage.

'Taking a swim.' Thank goodness her voice didn't waver. 'The question is, Idris, what you are doing here. This is private property and I don't recall inviting you in.' Petty but the words felt good. A small revenge for the way he had treated her all those years ago.

'I'm here to see the surr…' He stopped mid-sentence, his gaze dropping to her stomach, and incredulity stole over his face. 'You? *You're* the surrogate?'

Saskia raised her chin. 'I don't see how that's any of your business. I'm not supposed to be experiencing any stress so please leave and let me get on with my swim.'

He glared. 'Gladly. Only I need to speak to you. It's important.'

'Okay. Make it brief.'

'No, not out here. You need to be sat down. Dressed.' His gaze swept down her, impersonal, as if he had never seen her body before. Never touched her. Saskia's cheeks burned but she remained upright, head held high.

'You don't give the orders round here, Idris. You ask. Nicely.'

His gaze smouldered but he bit back whatever cutting retort sprang to his lips. 'Please,' he ground out. 'Saskia, this is important. Believe me, I wouldn't be here if it wasn't.'

She held his gaze, searching for answers within its darkness, fear uncoiling down her spine. Something was very, very wrong here. Why wasn't Idris in France? Where was Maya? Saskia nodded, slowly. 'Give me fifteen minutes. Everything takes a little longer right now.'

For the last couple of months Saskia had lived either in yoga pants or sheer voluminous kaftans, which made her look as if she were about to act as a sail in an am-dram version of *The Tempest* but, crucially, were cool and comfortable. Neither seemed right just now, instinct warning her that she needed more armour than casual, comfortable clothes would provide.

Luckily Maya had provided her with a designer pregnancy wardrobe fit for a princess. Saskia had pointed out that, confined to the villa as she was, she wouldn't have the opportunity to wear a tenth of the clothes but Maya had waved off her objections. 'You can keep them all and use them when you have your own baby, Sas,' she'd said. Saskia hadn't had the heart to tell her that having a baby of her own didn't figure anywhere in her plans, sensing Maya was buying her the wardrobe she herself wished she could have owned. So Saskia had accepted each gift with a smile and tried not to think about where on earth she would store several wardrobes full of unworn maternity clothes when she finally returned home.

She selected a pair of white cropped linen trousers and teamed them with a nude pink vest top, which gathered in a knot just below her breasts, the material flowing nicely over her bump. Many redheads eschewed pink, even as pale a shade as this, but Saskia loved the colour. She pulled her still-wet hair back into a loose plait and slipped her feet into a pair of flat sandals. She was ready.

Idris was here.

The enormity of what was happening hit her anew and Saskia reached out to the ornately carved bedpost for support. What on earth had brought him back to her after seven years? It was clear that he hadn't expected to see her; he'd looked just as thrown by the recognition as she had been.

Her lips tightened. She was a different person now. Strong, independent. A survivor. Just because Idris's kisses used to make her forget who she was didn't mean he had any power over her now. She had this situation in hand. She had to.

Summoning a confidence that wasn't quite real, yet not entirely fake, Saskia left her suite and slowly descended the villa's majestic staircase. The stairway led to the large central hallway from which all the other ground-floor rooms were situated. All marble and dark polished wood, it was lined with two impossibly long, armless couches. Idris lounged on the right-hand couch, seemingly completely at ease as he scrolled impatiently through his tablet. He didn't even raise his gaze to watch her as she walked carefully down the marble stairs.

One of the many occasional tables that were scattered around the villa had been brought to his side and a jug of coffee sat there along with a half-full cup. The aroma floated tantalisingly towards Saskia. Coffee was one of the many prohibited food and drinks she had agreed not to touch until three months after the baby was born and her duties had ended. Many she barely touched anyway—she didn't have the budget for shellfish, brie or wine—but coffee was her lifeline and she missed it every day; mint tea just didn't have the same effect.

As the thought flitted across her mind Hamid, the houseboy, pulled up a second table and placed a cup of the herbal beverage upon it. Suppressing a longing sigh, Saskia smiled her thanks. She made no move to sit, nor did she have any intention of standing in front of Idris and waiting for him to notice her. Instead she picked up the cup and walked away into her favourite sitting area, the smallest of the living rooms with stunning views of the pool and the sea beyond. She curled up on the couch, picked up a book and waited for Idris to come to her.

She didn't have to wait long. A smothered exclamation was followed by short sharp footsteps. '*Tiens*, there you are. Why didn't you let me know you were ready?'

Saskia hadn't taken in a word on the page but she still made a show of finishing her sentence before half closing the book and looking up with a mild smile. 'You looked busy. Take a seat, Idris, and let me know how I can help you.' There, she had established that this was her home and she was the one in charge.

To her surprise Idris didn't react with impatience or irritation. He sat down on the chair at right angles to her and leaned forwards before jumping up and striding across the room, his face set and eyes clouded. The premonition Saskia had felt in the pool returned, fear icy on her skin.

'What is it, Idris? Why are you here?'

He turned and the grief on his face clawed at her heart. 'There was an accident. Fayaz…' He stopped and swallowed.

'What kind of accident?'

'A car accident.'

'He will always drive too fast. Such a boy racer.' If she could keep chatting, keep the conversation light and inconsequential then she wouldn't have to hear the rest. Because of course there was more. Idris wouldn't have flown over from France for a minor injury. Nor would he have come here to tell her—to tell the unknown surrogate—in person.

'Saskia.' She could only sit paralysed while he walked back towards her, each deliberate, slow step echoing around her brain. He sat next to her, so familiar and yet a stranger and, to her increasing dread, took her hand in his. Once the simple touch of his hand would leave her incoherent and unable to think about anything but him, but right now she couldn't feel anything. All she could do was wait for the words she knew were coming.

'Saskia, the accident, it was a bad one. Fayaz didn't make it. Nobody did.'

Nobody? Her free hand crept down to her belly, whether to reassure the baby or herself she didn't know. 'Maya?' Her throat was so swollen she could barely croak the word out, but she knew that he heard her when his grip on her hand intensified.

'I'm sorry, Saskia. She was with him.'

She didn't move, didn't react, couldn't react, couldn't process anything he was saying. Fayaz and Maya. Such a golden couple; beautiful, wealthy, powerful sure but also caring and loving, and they had known their share of tragedy. Years of IVF and three miscarriages had left Maya utterly bereft—which was why she had come to Saskia.

Saskia's hand stilled on her belly. She pulled her other hand out of Idris's clasp and turned to him. 'The baby? What happens to their baby?'

CHAPTER TWO

IDRIS STARED UNSEEINGLY out at the sea. He needed to get back to Jayah. The funerals would be taking place in just a few hours' time and there were a hundred and one things demanding Idris's attention, but his business at the villa wasn't done. Not nearly. Saskia's question echoed round and round his mind. What happened to the baby? Orphaned before birth. His cousin's baby and, morally, the rightful heir.

But the burning question remained unanswered: was it the legal heir? Idris had no idea; which was why he was still kicking his heels at the villa, awaiting both the lawyer who had drawn up the surrogacy agreement and his great-uncle so that he could get their advice. Advice he was praying tied in with his own plans, because *if* the baby could inherit and *if* his great-uncle was prepared to take on the Regency until it was of age then Idris could return to France as soon as the mourning period was over.

He pushed away the guilt clenching his chest. Fayaz would have understood why he couldn't stay; he knew how alone Idris always felt in Dalmaya. How out of place. Set apart by his accent, his French upbringing. Tainted by the dishonour his mother had brought on her family, not just by her elopement but by her subsequent lifestyle. Fayaz knew how duty already ruled his life, knew how hard Idris had worked to restore the chateau, the vineyards, to make the Delacour name mean something again. He wouldn't expect Idris to put all that aside for a country that had never quite acknowledged him. Would he?

The all too familiar burden of heavy expectations descended onto his shoulders. Fayaz might not have expected Idris to put everything aside, but he would have known that it was almost impossible for Idris to turn away.

Almost…

At the back of his mind another question burned white hot. What was Saskia Harper doing here? Why on earth was she acting as Maya's surrogate? The guilt pulsed harder. He'd spent the last seven years doing his best not to think about Saskia, but occasionally he would see a flash of auburn hair, hear an imperious English accent and his heart would stutter to a stop, a tiny part of him hoping it might be her.

He hadn't expected to be so numb with grief when he did finally see her again that he had barely registered the shock of her presence.

The doctor's footsteps echoed through the hallway and Idris turned to the doorway, impatient for some answers. The midwife who worked full time at the villa had taken one look at Saskia and hustled her straight to bed, insisting that she be seen immediately by a doctor. The guilt pulsed again. Fayaz would expect him to do his best for his child *and* for its mother. 'How is she?'

The doctor took off his glasses and rubbed his eyes. 'As well as can be expected, Your Highness. A severe shock at any stage of pregnancy should be avoided if possible, but she's strong, healthy and has had the best possible care throughout. However, as a precaution, I've suggested bed rest for the rest of today and that she take it as easy as possible for the next few days. It's out of the question for her to attend the funerals, of course. She shouldn't be travelling.'

The funerals. Idris clenched his jaw and refused to acknowledge the grief beating down on him. There was no time, not now. 'Of course.'

'I'm leaving Nurse Wilson in charge. She has my personal number if there are any concerns. I'll come out straight away but I don't foresee any problems. Try and keep Sayeda Saskia calm, and make sure she eats something.' The doctor paused. 'I'm very sorry for your loss, Your Highness. Your cousin was a good man and Queen Maya deserved the happiness this baby would have brought her. I'll be back in the morning.'

Idris spent the next couple of hours sending emergency emails. Just because it felt as if he were standing in the eye of a storm, unable to move while events whirled around him, didn't mean he could neglect his own concerns. He closed his eyes briefly, picturing the weathered grey stone, the chateau turrets, the acres of slowly ripening vines. He'd made his home, made his mark at Chateau Delacour, knew every inch of soil, every man, woman and child in its environs. Last night he'd gone to bed expecting to wake up to another spring day, making sure he put some time aside to join the workers in the field as they carefully hoed and weeded the precious vines. What was the point of living in the glorious French countryside if he spent all his life in an office? Instead he'd awoken to a panicked call and his life had come to an abrupt halt. The vineyard felt like a lifetime, not a continent away.

He knew his managers could take charge of the vineyard and his export business until he returned and he made sure they had all the relevant authorisation to do so, warning them that he would likely be difficult to get hold of and so they should contact him only in an emergency. He stopped as he typed a reassuring message promising them he would be back as soon as possible—he just hoped he was telling them the truth. Meanwhile a flood of panicked emails flooded in from the various ministries all needing guidance. He told each one to carry on as usual, promising an announcement on the succession imminently. He hoped he was telling them the truth as well. It was a long, testing couple of hours and he was relieved to hear the car pull up heralding the advisors he needed.

'*Assalamu alaikum*, this way, please.' Idris gestured to the stairs. On the midwife's advice he had decided to hold the meeting in Saskia's rooms—the doctor had said she was to be kept quiet but she clearly had a stake in the subject under discussion and Idris sensed it would be far more stressful for her if she was left out.

The houseboy led them up the staircase and indicated the door leading to Saskia's apartments. Idris paused, the reality of the situation hitting him anew. Fayaz was gone—and Saskia was here. Here in Dalmaya. Not quite his territory but close enough to discombobulate him with her unexpected presence.

Her bedroom was huge, the outside wall made entirely of glass, doors leading out to a large terrace filled with plants and shaded seats overlooking the sea. The room was decorated in soothing shades of blue and cream; a gigantic bed with ornately carved wooden bedposts sat on a platform at one end of the room, a seating area grouped at the other. Two doors were slightly ajar, and Idris could see they led into a dressing area and a bathroom. Refreshments had been placed onto the coffee table and Saskia was already lying on one of the three couches arranged around it. She smiled wanly at the lawyer as he greeted her and extended her hand to Idris's great-uncle.

'Please excuse me for not getting up but I have been ordered not to move.'

'No apologies needed.' The elderly man bowed over her hand. 'Sheikh Malik Al Osman. It's an honour to meet you, Sheikha Saskia.'

Idris started at the honorary title, nodding curtly at Saskia and taking the seat farthest away from her. A quick glance showed him how pale she was under her tan, the pain in her eyes reflecting the pain he saw in the mirror. He ruthlessly pressed on; there was far more at stake here than personal feelings. 'I don't have much time,' he said, opening proceedings briskly. 'So let's get going. Can somebody explain just what is going on here and why nobody knows anything about this baby?'

The lawyer nodded, setting his briefcase on the table and taking out a sheaf of papers. 'I acted for Their Majesties in this matter so maybe I should start. You have to understand, Sheikh Idris, that legally surrogacy and adoption are still grey areas here in Dalmaya. Historically if a woman couldn't conceive she would simply raise a family member's child as her own—either a sister's or cousin's or a fellow wife's child, and that child would be considered hers. Plus any child she bears during marriage is legally her husband's regardless of actual biological fatherhood; that goes for any child she raises for someone else too.'

Idris frowned. 'So all Maya had to do was call herself the baby's mother and the baby became hers and Fayaz's without any need to adopt it legally?'

'*Traditionally* that's all that they had to do. Of course, by using a surrogate they had ensured the baby was Fayaz's biological child anyway, but because Sayeda Saskia is a British citizen, and to make sure there was no confusion in the future, they were planning to adopt the baby in the British courts as well.'

'So why the secrecy? You said it yourself, raising someone else's child is culturally acceptable and the baby is Fayaz's biologically, so there should be no quibbling over inheritance.'

'Your grandfather's reforms and his subsequent decision to take just one wife, a stance followed by his son and grandson, hasn't been popular amongst traditionalists, partly because it has greatly reduced the number of potential heirs in the Al Osman senior branch. Your grandfather had just two children and his only son died while Fayaz was still a child. If it was known that the Queen couldn't conceive there would have been great pressure on Fayaz to take a second wife.'

'Maya felt like such a failure,' Saskia said, staring down at her hands. 'She put herself through hell. IVF after IVF, three terrible miscarriages. She knew how important it was that Fayaz had an heir...she knew that you didn't want...' She came to a halt, flashing one quick glance over at him. He'd forgotten just how disconcerting her green eyes were, no hint of hazel or blue diluting them.

'How many people know about this?'

'I have known from the start. Fayaz discussed it with me before they went down the surrogacy route,' Sheikh Malik said. 'As head of the junior branch of the family he wanted to make sure I had no objections, that there would be no repercussions later on. The staff here know, any lawyers involved in the adoption and surrogacy agreement and certain medical staff here and in the UK. They all signed binding non-disclosure agreements, of course. The heads of the Privy Council are now aware after this morning's meeting, but they can all be relied on to keep quiet, if it's for the good of the country. But do we want to keep it quiet? If Fayaz has a son and heir then surely we need to let people know.'

'Or a daughter,' Saskia said quietly, her hands back on her stomach. Idris could hardly drag his eyes away from her slim, long fingers as they stroked the bump; the gesture seemed automatic, maybe as much comfort for mother as for child. But Saskia was only the mother until birth… Idris watched her hands in their rhythmic pattern. No child should be born motherless. Even his own beautiful, selfish, careless mother had been around sometimes for kisses and bedtime stories. Occasionally even two nights in a row.

Of course there had been the many weeks he had barely seen her at all.

'The problem is—' The lawyer's voice recalled Idris's attention back to the matter at hand. He tore his gaze away from Saskia and concentrated on the papers spread out over the coffee table. 'A baby's paternity in this country is proven only in two ways. Either the father claims the child as his, which is what Fayaz intended…'

'What about the surrogacy agreement?' Saskia asked. 'Doesn't that prove Fayaz was going to claim the baby?'

The lawyer shook his head. 'Surrogacy isn't recognised here. The only way Fayaz could posthumously be recognised as the father would be if you had been married to him.'

Idris's heart stopped for one long, painful second

as he processed the words. There was no way out. If Fayaz couldn't legally be proven as the father, if the child wasn't legitimised, then it couldn't inherit. Which meant the Kingship fell heavily onto Idris's own shoulders. A burden he had never asked for and certainly never wanted. He glanced out of the window at the relentless blue and his chest ached as he recalled the myriad colours of the French late spring: greens and lavender and red.

'In that case who does it belong to?' Saskia's voice cut into his thoughts. 'Isn't that the most important thing we need to decide? Who is going to raise this baby? Time isn't on our side.'

Idris stared at her. 'What do you mean?'

'I *mean*,' she said, emphasising every word, 'its parents have died. It's due in six weeks and it needs a family regardless of whether it can inherit the throne or not. Could another branch of the family adopt it? Would that be what Fayaz would want? Do we know? I mean, that surrogacy agreement covered everything down to what vitamins I should take pre- and post-pregnancy. I can't believe Fayaz didn't have a contingency plan if something like this should happen.'

The lawyer nodded. 'He had named a guardian for the baby.'

'Who?' Saskia and Idris spoke together.

The lawyer's gaze shifted to Idris. 'His cousin, Sheikh Idris Delacour.'

'Moi?'

'Him?' Again the two of them were in unison. Idris looked over at Saskia. He'd spent the last seven years doing his best to forget about her. How could he raise a child that was half hers? A child who would remind him of its mother every second of every day?

How could he raise a child at all? His mother said all he cared about was the vineyard, about work, and for once she had a point.

'Let me see that.' He held out his hand for the sheaf of papers and scanned them quickly. Even through the dense legalese Fayaz's intentions were clear. If anything happened to Fayaz, then Idris was to be guardian to any children until their twenty-first birthday. Idris swallowed. Fayaz was just like their grandfather, intent on making sure Idris was part of the family even if he was French by birth and name. But Fayaz couldn't have meant to make him responsible for a motherless newborn; he knew nothing about children—and by the incredulous look on Saskia's face she was thinking exactly the same thing.

He turned his concentration back to the papers, flicking through them until he reached the surrogacy contract. Saskia was right, it *was* thorough, covering everything from diet to exercise to location, stating she was to travel to Dalmaya as soon as the pregnancy was confirmed and stay until three months after the birth in order to provide nutrition for the baby. It took every bit of self-possession he had not to look up at that, not to look over at her full, ripe breasts. He took a deep breath and continued to read.

All her medical bills paid, of course, accommodation, clothes and food provided throughout the timespan of the agreement, school fees paid—school fees for who? His eyebrows flew up in unspoken query, only to lower as he read the allowance made to her every week. Bound to the villa, every need catered for, she was going to be pocketing a nice profit by the end of the contract. He turned the page and stopped, rereading the words again before tossing the contract contemptuously onto the table as he glared at Saskia.

'You're being paid for this?' It took everything he had not to spit the words out. His cousin and his glowing wife, desperate for a baby. How hard must it have been for Maya to watch Saskia do so easily what she couldn't, knowing that the baby was just a way for the surrogate mother to make money?

Saskia flushed. 'That is none of your business.'

'I think you'll find it is very much my business,' he reminded her silkily and her colour heightened. 'I don't know why I'm surprised. You always did like to play games. But this isn't a game, Saskia. This was Fayaz and Maya's life!'

Her colour was still high but her eyes flashed as she shifted. 'Maya came to me, asked me to do this. I *didn't* play games or negotiate on payment. I took what was offered, yes, why wouldn't I? I have given this baby over a year of my life. Restricted my diet, my liberty, taken fertility drugs, undergone invasive procedure after invasive procedure to give this baby the best possible start in life. So don't throw the fact I'm to be paid in my face as if it makes me some kind of whore. Of course I was happy to help Maya, but I was in no position to give her a year of my life for love alone.'

'It's not a payment as such, that's illegal under British law and the baby was conceived in the UK,' the lawyer interjected quickly. 'It's compensation for Miss Harper's loss of income and freedom. The compensation is to be paid at the end of the contract if every condition has been adhered to and if Sayeda Saskia ensures that she prioritises the baby's well-being until it reaches the age of three months.'

Taking a deep breath to quell his anger, Idris turned

to his great-uncle. 'I know what my grandfather's will says, but surely my name, my heritage precludes me from taking the throne? Isn't there anyone more qualified in another branch of the family? Your branch?'

Sheikh Malik shook his head. 'Not without tremendous upheaval and turmoil, Idris. The kind of turmoil your grandfather spent his life trying to ensure the country would never go through again. Yes, your father is French but more importantly you're the grandson of the Great Reformer. I don't think the people will reject you. Your name doesn't matter but if it worries you it's easy enough to change it to Delacour Al Osman.' He paused, leaning forward, his gaze intent on Idris. 'I can't force you to accept the throne, but, Idris, I can and will beg you to. For your grandfather's sake, for your cousin's sake, for your country.'

A great weariness descended on Idris. His destiny was as clear as it was unwanted. He'd never appreciated his life properly before, the old chateau lovingly restored piece by piece, the vineyards, finally back in profit, and making wines he was proud to put his name to, the family coffers filling again despite his parents' best efforts. It was hard work involving long hours but it was satisfying and he was in control. Best of all it was quiet. No drama, no press, no obligations beyond those of the people who worked for him. How could he swap that for life in the spotlight, an entire country reliant on his success? For a child who wasn't his?

How could he not? His parents showed him all too well the consequences of living for nothing but self. Thanks to them he had grown up always worrying how the next bill would be paid, where they would be living next, even what they would be eating that night. Thankfully he had been able to escape to his grandfathers, to the two men who had never met but would have liked and respected each other, if their paths had ever crossed. The men who had taught him that duty and honour and responsibility weren't burdens but the measure of a man.

Sometimes he envied his mother, her carefree waltz through life, her refusal to be bound by convention. But such a path was selfish, had consequences for all those around.

A King's life wasn't his, he knew that all too well. His own needs, his own desires, his own likes always second to duty. And Idris saw his duty all too clearly. All of it.

His mind raced as he ruthlessly ousted all emotions from his mind, concentrating on the cold, hard facts, looking for the path ahead. First, it was clearly in the baby's best interests to have a mother's care right from birth. Second, he, Idris, was the *legal* heir, whether he liked it or not. But, third, at the same time the unborn baby was the *rightful* heir. Fourth, he was said baby's guardian. The pieces began to fall into place one by one.

What had the lawyer said? That if a man was married to the mother when a child was born then he was automatically that child's legal father regardless of actual paternity? He looked over at the other man. 'Let me get this straight. If I marry Sayeda Saskia then the baby will be my child, my heir, in both law and in the eyes of the world.'

The lawyer's words were drowned out by Saskia's indignant, 'There is no way I am marrying you, Idris Delacour, not if you were the last man alive!' But Idris saw the nod and he knew what he had to do. For Fayaz, for the country, for the baby. He had to marry the only woman he had ever come close to loving. The woman he had walked away from. He had to marry Saskia Harper.

CHAPTER THREE

IT WAS ALL very well being told not to allow herself to become agitated but how was Saskia supposed to stay calm when Idris dropped a bombshell more explosive than she could possibly have imagined, and then calmly wrapped up the meeting and disappeared as if she had meekly fallen into line with his insane plans? Marry Idris? The man who had ripped her heart and self-esteem to shreds and then stomped on them without mercy? The man who had let her down at the lowest point in her life?

'Sorry, baby,' Saskia told it that sleepless night. 'I know it's scary now that Maya isn't here to look after you, but marrying Idris isn't the best thing for either of us. I'm not ready to be a mother yet, and you deserve more than that. He's going to be King. He can give you everything you need.'

But he couldn't give the baby a mother who would love it unconditionally—and she knew that was the only thing Maya would ask of her. Saskia's eyes filled and she hurriedly blinked back the tears, trying to focus on her indignation instead. The only positive thing to come out of this whole mess was that her anger with Idris helped her to manage the shock of losing Maya and Fayaz. She was so busy thinking of one hundred ways to tell him that she would rather marry Jabba the Hutt than him that the grief had released some of its painful grip from her chest—although she did keep reaching for her phone ready to text Maya with a planned, clever comeback, only for the grief to descend again with all its painful intensity when she remembered she would never be able to text her again.

Not that she had had an opportunity to test even one of her scathing put-downs on Idris yet. Twenty-four hours had passed with no word from him and she had no way to contact him. Saskia stared out of the window. Of course, he had been a little busy burying his cousin and closest friend. She choked back a sob, the lump back in her throat. She wished she had had the opportunity to say goodbye too. No, that wasn't true. She wished more than anything that she could have handed her newborn baby over to Maya and seen the moment her friend fell in love with her much-wanted child.

Yes, she had agreed to be a surrogate for the money, she had never pretended her motives were anything more altruistic, but she had also wanted to be the one to make her friend's dreams come true. At least Maya had died knowing she would soon be a mother. Saskia twisted her hands together. Would Maya have wanted Saskia to raise her baby for her? She knew how much Saskia had sacrificed already raising Jack; surely she wouldn't have expected her to sacrifice more?

'His Highness Sheikh Idris Delacour Al Osman,' the houseboy announced and Saskia jumped. She hadn't even heard the car pull up, too absorbed in her thoughts. She turned, glad she had dressed ready for his return whenever it might be, in a severely cut grey linen shift dress, her hair coiled in a businesslike knot on the top of her head.

She sat upright in her chair—no more reclining, no more weakness—and folded her ankles and hands. Poised, collected and ready to do battle. But the cold words she had prepared faded as soon as Idris entered the room. He was grey with fatigue, shadows pronounced under his eyes and the grief lines cut deep. She held out her hand with no more thought than the need to comfort someone suffering as she suffered, only to drop it as he walked straight past it as if it weren't there. She leaned back and regarded him, doing her best to hide her humiliation and anger. How dared he treat her like that when he was the one who had let her down at the most vulnerable moment in her life? *She* should be the one shunning *him*.

Idris stood, back to her, staring out of the windows. Saskia regarded him for a few moments before turning to the houseboy and requesting some tea and refreshments. She sat back, displaying a composure she was a long way from feeling, and waited. Several long minutes passed before he spoke, the tea served and the houseboy dismissed, Saskia not moving or speaking, refusing to be the one to break first. Finally Idris shifted, although he still didn't face her.

'I've discussed our marriage with the heads of the Privy Council. They agree a big royal wedding is not in the country's best interests right now. We're still in the mourning period and your condition will give rise to the kind of speculation it's best to avoid. However, time is clearly not on our side so the consensus is for a quiet wedding here as soon as possible. The lawyer is drawing up the paperwork right now and we are thinking the day after tomorrow for the ceremony. In accordance with Dalmayan law it is simply the signing of a contract. Traditionally the elder of your house would negotiate the contract for you, but my grandfather decreed that women now act for themselves. As time and secrecy are of the essence the lawyer who drew up the surrogacy will advise you and I suggest you go over the contract with him before the ceremony.'

Saskia listened to every crazy word, her mind busily coming up with—and discarding—several considered responses pointing out exactly why this was such a bad idea but in the end she settled for a simple 'No.'

Idris turned slowly. 'No?'

'No. No to the wedding. No to marriage. No to spending any more time with you than I have to.'

His mouth compressed. 'Believe me, Saskia, if there was another way…'

'You don't need me. You're the baby's guardian regardless of whether I marry you or not. Marry someone else. Someone you can bear to be in the same room with.'

'This isn't about you and me. This is about what's right.'

'Oh, don't be so sanctimonious. The last thing Fayaz or Maya would want is for *us* of all people to be trapped into marriage with each other. Not for us and not for the baby.'

'And the baby's right to inherit?'

'If you adopt it…'

'You heard the lawyer. Formal adoption is still an unknown process in Dalmaya.'

'Well, then marry someone else and adopt the baby quietly, like Maya intended to.'

'You want me to woo and marry someone in less than six weeks?'

'You're about to be King. The kingdom must be full of women desperate to fall at your feet and into your arms.' Funny to think she was one of those women once—and she hadn't needed a title, just one of his rare smiles.

'There can be no ambiguity about the baby's heritage. No, Saskia, this is the best way. The only way.'

'Then you are in trouble because I am not going to marry you.' She clasped her hands to stop them shaking and waited, heart hammering.

There's nothing he can do, she told herself. *Dalmaya is a civilised country. He's not going to drag you to the altar by your hair.*

She stared straight at Idris, defiant but a little confused by the look on his face. He didn't look angry or upset, he looked amused, bordering on smug. Her throat dried.

'You signed a contract.'

'To have a baby.'

'*Non*, you agreed to a lot more than that. You agreed to do whatever is in the baby's best interests until he or she is three months old and, if required to *in extremis*, to come to its aid in later life.'

Saskia blinked. 'Yes, but that's because Fayaz and Maya wanted me to express milk for the baby for the first three months so I need to stay here for those three months and adhere to the right diet. That's all that the *in the best interests* part means.'

'That's not what it says,' he said softly, gaze still intent on hers. 'You did read the contract before signing it, didn't you?'

'Of course, and my lawyer took me through every clause…' She halted. That clause was written exactly the way Idris had phrased it. They didn't know what would happen, her lawyer had explained. What if the baby needed a blood transfusion and she, not Fayaz, was the right match? Or, later on, a kidney, unlikely as that might be? Even a donor sibling? The three months post birth she was glad to agree to; it was an opportunity to recover from pregnancy and birth in comfort and peace. The statistical chance of the *in extremis* clause being invoked had been low enough for her not to be concerned—compensation would be offered commensurate with whatever was needed and, besides, of course she would want to help if it was within her power to do so. 'It doesn't mean what you're implying.'

'Oh?' He raised an eyebrow. 'The baby doesn't need a mother for its first three months? Being orphaned before birth isn't *in extremis* enough? Tell me, Saskia, what have you been doing since the last time I saw you? Apart from dropping out from university?'

Her hands curled into tight fists. How could he be so dismissive? Act as if they hadn't once been, if not in love, so very close to falling off that cliff? Maybe it had just been her, so besotted she hadn't noticed how little he felt for her. But for all his faults, for all his arrogance, she had never known Idris Delacour be deliberately cruel. Even that last time…she hadn't actually managed to tell him about her father's death when he sent her away.

Surely Maya and Fayaz had filled him in on what had happened to her, told him about her father? She'd assumed so. But if he hadn't known she was their choice of surrogate, hadn't known she was in Dalmaya, then maybe not. Thinking about it, they had always been very careful not to discuss Idris with her beyond mentioning that he had achieved his dream of renovating the chateau and the vineyards. Her pulse began to race as she took in his politely contemptuous expression. He couldn't know, not about her father's death, not about

Jack. After all, she hadn't even known of Jack's existence when they were together.

She lifted her chin. 'This and that.' If he didn't know about Jack then she wasn't going to enlighten him. The less he knew about her life, her circumstances, the better. The less ammunition he would have.

'No husband? Fiancé? Significant other? Career? I thought not. I'm offering you it all on a plate, Saskia, a family, a home, a position that comes with all the luxuries and money a girl like you needs to get by.'

She wouldn't cry. Wouldn't give him the satisfaction of even a chin wobble. 'You know nothing about a girl like me.'

'*Non?* Well, I suppose I have the rest of my life to find out.'

'The answer is still no. You can sue me, Idris. See what people think about the King of Dalmaya suing a woman into becoming his wife. I can take that kind of humiliation, can you?'

His eyes were hard and flat. That shot had gone home. He'd always been abominably proud. 'I don't need to sue you, Saskia. If you don't marry me and legitimise the baby then the lawyer agrees you have broken the *in extremis* clause and the first three months agreement. We won't owe you a red cent. You'll leave here not a penny the richer for your year and a bit's hard work.' His eyes flicked contemptuously to the side table laden with little pastries and fruits.

The world stilled and stopped. No money? No money meant no house, no university, no way of clawing herself out of the exhausting cycle she had found herself repeating over and over for the last seven years. No money meant a return to long hours and mind-numbing work, to low wages and choosing between food and heating.

To damp flats. No money meant no security for Jack… She couldn't breathe, the lump in her throat outsized only by the heavy stone in her chest. She couldn't do it all again. She couldn't…

Somehow, she had no idea how, she managed to take in a breath, only her whitened knuckles giving away her inner turmoil. She *could* do it. She'd done it before. She would have no choice but to pick herself up once again.

But not without a fight. 'I'll talk to my lawyer.'

'You do that,' he said affably. 'I can afford to fight this all the way. Can you say the same, Saskia? Daddy must be keeping you short if you've resorted to surrogacy and you've been off the party circuit for a while. Will any of your boyfriends pick up the tab?'

The casual, contemptuous mention of her father was like a physical blow but she didn't waver, keeping her voice low and cold. 'Don't you worry about me.'

'You'll be a single mother as well. That's not the kind of accessory men look for in their dates.'

Her gaze snapped up to meet his. There was no humour in his dark eyes, just a searing contempt. 'What do you mean?'

He shrugged. 'The lawyer was quite clear. Under Dalmayan law there's no way of proving that the child is Fayaz's. I don't have any obligation to take in a child of unknown origin.'

'The agreement. His DNA…' But she remembered the lawyer's words as clearly as Idris did.

'Inadmissible.'

'Not in the UK.'

'Saskia, we're not in the UK.'

'You'd turn your back on your cousin's child?'

'This country is going through enough right now. I wasn't born here or brought up here. My first language is French, my surname is French. My mother ran away surrounded by the biggest scandal of the last century. That's the legacy I inherit. I need to be seen as committed to Dalmaya. The last thing I need is a motherless baby who isn't mine muddling up the succession. Now, I'm willing to marry you, legitimise the baby and make it my heir. But it's all or nothing, Saskia. Pick wisely.'

Go to hell.

The words were so tempting but she reined them in while she desperately searched for a way out, a way to reach him. Her earlier thought ran through her brain like a track on repeat, reminding her that the Idris she had known before wasn't cruel. Single-minded, yes. Definitely ambitious. But not cruel. Not until the last time she'd seen him.

But that man, that man who had turned his back on her, he was capable of turning his back on the baby too, she was almost sure. Almost…it was a slim word to hang her hopes on to. Could she risk it?

If he was in earnest then she wouldn't just be returning to the UK penniless, she'd be returning with a baby. A baby would make finding a job, a place to live so very, very much harder…

And of course there was Jack. She'd promised him a better life. Could she drag him back to an even more difficult childhood than the one he'd left? He'd never complained before but he'd never known another way before.

'Saskia!' A voice broke through her thoughts and she looked up. Was it that time already? She'd meant to keep Jack well away from Idris but it was too late. Her brother raced through the marble hallway, dropping his bag in the middle of the room as he kicked off his shoes. His au pair followed, picking up his discarded belongings as she went. How quickly he'd adjusted to the heat and the space and the staff. How could she take him back to an inadequately heated one-bedroom flat?

He skidded to a halt by her chair. Ignoring Idris's raised brow, she held out her arms for the cuddle her brother still greeted her with. 'Jack, how was your day, tiger?'

'Good. I scored three goals during playtime.'

'Three goals, huh? Good to see you're learning something in that fancy school of yours. Jack, I want you to meet someone. This is Idris. I used to…' She faltered. 'We knew each other when I was younger. He is Fayaz's cousin.'

Jack turned, a little shyly, but stuck out his hand. 'Pleased to meet you.'

Idris threw her a startled glance as he shook Jack's hand. 'Pleased to meet you too, Jack. Are you over visiting Saskia?' But his keen eyes were scanning Jack and Saskia knew he had noted the school uniform, the au pair, the houseboy standing to one side with a tray filled with milk and cookies. All the signs that Jack was a permanent member of the household.

'No.' Jack sounded surprised. 'I live here.'

'You live here?' His brows had snapped together and he was looking at Jack assessingly.

'Jack is my brother and I am his guardian,' Saskia interjected smoothly. 'Jack, go and have your milk and cookies in the kitchen, okay? Then I think Husain has offered to give you a swimming lesson.'

'Really? Cool!' And he was gone in a blur of elbows and calves.

'He lives with you?'

'Yes.'

'Where's his mother?'

She shrugged. 'I'm not quite sure. She *was* in Brazil last I heard but she doesn't keep in contact.'

'Your father?'

'Dead. Look, Jack is none of your business so let's…'

If the news of her father's death surprised him he hid it well. 'If your brother lives with you then he is very much my business. When we are married…'

'You haven't listened to a word I've said, have you? I am not marrying you, Idris. Not in two days' time, not ever.' But although her words and tone were defiant despair flowed through her. There was no happy ending here. Her dreams of returning to England in just a few months ready to restart her degree and with enough money to buy a small house somewhere within commuting distance of London had turned into a nightmare. Either she returned back to the same hardship Maya had rescued her from—only this time with a baby in tow—or she stayed and married Idris. There would be no money worries if she chose the latter. But there would be no hope of escape either.

Idris reached into his pocket and pulled out a small card, which he handed to her. Numbly she took it, barely glancing at the plain black type on the crisp white background. 'My number. If you change your mind call me tomorrow. If not then I will organise a plane to take you and your brother back to London as soon as possible. The choice is yours.'

And then he was gone. Saskia put the card down, her hands trembling so much she wasn't sure she would ever be able to make them stop. She wasn't going to give in. Never.

Tucking Jack in wasn't easy; she couldn't bend over the bed any more. Instead Saskia had to perch on the side of the bed while she read to him. Saskia could forget her worries for a short while as she read the story of a boy wizard and his adventures out loud, doing all the voices as instructed.

'At least I never had to sleep under the stairs,' Jack said as she closed the book and laid it on the bedside table.

'Not up to now,' Saskia agreed.

'When we go home, will you have a bedroom too?' Jack had always thought it most unfair that he had had a room of his own while Saskia had slept on a sofa bed in the flat's all-purpose living and dining room. But it had been an impossible conundrum. The temping agency she had worked for supplied offices around London's West End. The wages were very good for a temp job but to get into work for just before nine, to pay as little as possible on transport and to ensure she could fit in with the childminder's hours, Saskia had had to live as close to central London as she could afford. Which had meant compromising on space. The exorbitantly expensive, tiny new-build flat would have been bijou for one person; for a family of two, one of whom was an active growing boy, it was oppressively small. It had, however, been home but she had given up her rental agreement when she'd left England. Who knew where the two of them would end up?

The three of them…unless Idris was bluffing. But the coldness in his eyes had given her no hope of that.

Thank goodness Maya had insisted that she be paid an allowance—and thank goodness there had never been anything to spend it on. With some careful budgeting—and she was an expert at that—she could keep herself, Jack and the baby for six months. *Where* she was going to keep them was a whole other matter. London was out of the question financially. But London was all she knew, except for nine months spent in Oxford a lifetime ago.

'A bedroom of my own? I hope so.'

'And will we have a garden? With a footie goal and a basketball hoop and space for me to ride a bike?' He was drowsy now. This was the way he always fell asleep, talking about all the things they would have once their stay in Dalmaya was over. He wasn't greedy, he didn't want video games and gadgets, just space to run around and play. Saskia brushed the hair back from his forehead, her heart aching. He deserved to be able to play.

'That's the plan.'

'I wish we could have a pool like we have here. Dan's dad said he would teach us to ride and to sail, but I won't be here much longer.' Dan was his best friend and Jack had spent a lot of time at his house, although due to the secrecy surrounding the surrogacy he had never invited any of his friends to the villa. Another thing she had promised him: a home open to anyone he wanted. 'Can I learn to ride horses and to sail when we get home?'

'I'm not sure about that. It depends where we end up.'

'I'll miss the sun. And the sea. And the sand. I like it here. I wish we could stay…' And he was gone. Saskia didn't move, continuing to stroke his hair, watching his face, mobile even in sleep.

Funny to remember how resentful she'd been when she'd realised there was no one else to care for him, that along with the shame and the debts and the mess her father had bequeathed her, there was a toddler who needed clothing and feeding and taking care of. If she hadn't taken him in her life would have taken a very different turn; she would probably have taken her degree, got a job. She wouldn't have lived the gilded life she had enjoyed before her father's suicide; those circles had closed to her as soon as his embezzlement had been discovered. But she would have found something approximating her original plans of a career in the media, a shared flat in Notting Hill, parties at the weekend, skiing in winter and beaches in summer.

Instead she had spent her days filing, answering phones, typing up reports, eating her packed lunch on a bench in a city square, shopping in sales and charity shops. No holidays anywhere, weekends spent exploring London's abundance of free museums and city parks. She knew every exhibit in the Natural History Museum, every room, every sign.

She couldn't remember when resentment had turned to acceptance and then to love. Couldn't remember the day she'd looked at Jack and seen not a burden, but a gift. The day she had started to be grateful for what she had, not what she had lost.

Hauling herself to her feet, Saskia adjusted Jack's covers. He looked so well; no longer pale and over the winter he'd escaped the hacking cough he usually caught in the damp London cold. The dry desert air agreed with him; he'd grown inches, filled out a little, and he loved the international school he now attended. He was going to find it hard to adjust going back, especially when the promised new home didn't materialise and she was preoccupied with a newborn baby.

Saskia went straight to her room, opening the sliding doors and stepping out onto her terrace. The moon was bright and round, its reflection on the sea offering her a path to who knew where. If only she could get into one of the boats moored on the wooden pier and follow its enticing, silvery road. She leant on the balcony and breathed in, enjoying the faint sea breeze that cooled the warm, desert night.

She had agreed to become a surrogate to give Jack a better life. But, damn him, Idris was right. As soon as the baby had been implanted in her womb she had taken on an obligation to put him or her first as long as they were dependent on her. She had worked so hard not to get too attached to the baby, to remember she wasn't its mother, merely its caretaker, but of course she loved it. It was half her. She felt it move, hiccup, knew when it was sleeping and when it was restless.

Didn't the baby deserve a better life too? The life it was supposed to have? It was supposed to be the Prince or Princess of Dalmaya. To grow up surrounded by the sea and the desert, to be loved and cosseted and so very much wanted. And that life was still within her power to bequeath.

Jack could learn to sail and ride, stay at the school he liked so much, keep growing stronger and healthier.

And she? She could endure…

Slowly Saskia reached into her pocket and pulled out the white card with Idris's name and number on it. She stared at it, her mouth dry and her hands numb. Married to Idris. No university, no home of her own, instead a life with a man who despised her. Who she despised.

A life that would provide for the two children in her care.

She had told herself that she had a choice but, really, she had no choice at all. Fumbling, she reached for her phone and, blinking back the tears, dialled.

CHAPTER FOUR

THE YEAR SASKIA turned eight she was a bridesmaid for her friend's elder sister. The wedding was held in the village church and afterwards the whole congregation had walked in a joyful procession along the narrow lane to Saskia's house, where her father had allowed a marquee to be erected in the old manor house's extensive gardens. It was a perfect wedding and small Saskia, starry eyed, vowed that one day she would have one just like it. Of course the manor house had been sold to pay off her father's creditors and she had given up on romantic dreams a long time ago. Still, she had never imagined that she would get married while heavily pregnant to a man who disliked her and although she had no desire for white lace or ivory organza the calf-length, long-sleeved black dress screamed funeral rather than wedding—which seemed fitting enough.

The lawyer had spent the afternoon with her, once more taking her through a contract clause by clause, although as this one was written in Arabic Saskia knew she was putting a lot of trust in him; she could be setting her name to anything. The contract went on and on, detailing expected duties, allowances, long lists she could barely take in. One thing stood out: the marriage contract pragmatically contained provisions for a divorce with generous allowances for both herself and any children resulting from the marriage. An escape clause. It didn't quite lift the suffocation from her lungs or the heaviness from her heart but at least she would be dry eyed when she signed her marriage contract.

'Sayeda Saskia, they are waiting for you.' Leena, her maid, stood at her bedroom door, her eyes bright with excitement. The staff seemed to view the whole secret wedding as wildly romantic and she didn't like to disabuse them.

'*Shokran*, Leena, I'll be down shortly.' She paused. 'Actually, could you please ask Sheikh Idris to step up here for a moment?'

'You want to see him alone? In your bedroom? Before the wedding?' Her maid's eyes widened in shock.

It was a little too late to worry about incurring bad luck or risking her reputation—after all, she was already heavily pregnant. What else could happen? 'You can leave the door open and wait in the corridor.' That should be sufficient chaperonage. She sank back onto the sofa and awaited the arrival of her soon-to-be husband.

She didn't have to wait long. The sound of his decisive tread reached her within two minutes of sending Leena for him and within seconds he stood at the door of her room, unfairly devastating in a traditional high collared cream tunic embroidered with gold thread and matching loose trousers. Saskia's heart thumped and despite herself she felt the old sweet tug of attraction low in her belly.

How could this still happen? She knew exactly who Idris Delacour was: a man who had no compunction about blackmailing a vulnerable woman, hijacking her life with no care for the consequences. But somehow her body was out of step with her mind. She noted his every detail without trying: the cut of his cheekbones, the stubble grazing his jaw, the quizzical slant of his brow, the coiled strength in his stance. His body had filled out since university, no longer a boy's rangy torso but a man's body. One used to hard work. Strong, capable.

'You didn't need to make such an effort,' she said, her mouth dry.

He cast her plain dress a contemptuous glance. 'One of us had to.'

Ignoring his cutting tone took every ounce of self-control she had. Summoning a smile from goodness knew where, she waved a hand at the chair opposite her. 'Will you sit?'

Idris didn't take the offered chair; instead he stayed leaning against the door, his arms folded. 'What can I do for you? Or have you decided you don't want to go through with it after all?' He wasn't sure whether he would be more furious or more delighted if she changed her mind about the wedding.

'Do you want me to change my mind?'

He didn't dignify her with a response. 'Saskia, my uncle, his wife and the lawyer are downstairs waiting for you. If you have cold feet…'

'I need to know what this marriage entails,' she cut in. 'What it is you expect of me. And I need to know what I can expect from you.'

'You read the contract?'

'No, it was a little tricky seeing as it is written in Arabic, but it has been read to me. Idris, I don't want to know about clauses and agreements. I want to know about you and me. About our marriage and your expectations.'

'My expectations?' He drawled the word out, allowing a cold smile to curve his mouth. 'You don't have to worry, Saskia. We may be married but I have no intention of consummating our marriage at any point. Your *honour...*' he put a faint stress on the last word and watched the flush spread across her pale cheeks '...is quite safe with me. I have no interest in rekindling our past relationship.'

Liar, his conscience whispered. Saskia Harper had been a pretty girl but she had grown into a beautiful woman. The strawberry blonde hair had darkened to a bright auburn, a colour that reminded him of the grapevines back home in France as autumn fell. She was slightly tanned, a few more freckles sprinkled across her nose, her cheeks, and her body matured and ripened. But she had changed more than physically; Saskia had always been marked by her utter confidence. No nervous freshman, she had arrived in Oxford looking as if she fully expected the world and everything in it to fall at her feet—and they had. Idris had instantly placed her in the category of privileged girls who treated Oxford not as an education but as a launch into society, a place to meet influential people and date—and marry—influential men. Her instant friendship with Maya had made it hard for him to avoid her, but, despite the naturally flirtatious way she had treated everyone, he had been immune to her enchantment.

Or so he'd thought. Looking back, he'd been a little too smug about his immunity, a little too aware of her conquests, a little too surprised to find her in the library that Saturday afternoon, struggling with her essay on Marlowe, frustrated because she'd desperately wanted to impress a notoriously difficult tutor. After he had talked it through with her, Marlowe's immortal words had made sense in a way they never had before.

O, thou art fairer than the evening air
Clad in the beauty of a thousand stars

A woman like Saskia could launch one thousand ships, her beauty and intelligence and the depths he spied under that confident exterior utterly beguiling. Utterly dangerous. But in the end, just like Faustus's creation, the woman he'd thought he'd seen was just an illusion.

This new, older Saskia was no pushover either, but she didn't look as if she expected life to roll over at her feet any more. There was a hardness in the green eyes that hinted at past hurts.

'No, Idris. I'm not even remotely concerned with your sleeping arrangements.' That voice though! Still clear and cold, each word spoken with precision in her most English of accents, like a lady dowager in a breeches and bonnets film. 'I want to know how this works day to day.'

'How this works? You're going to be the Queen, Saskia.' And he the King. The words still sounded absurd, the whole situation unreal. He, Idris Delacour, a King, with all the pomp and circumstance and responsibility and lack of privacy it entailed. His chest tightened. He wasn't ready. He didn't think he would ever be ready.

Idris glanced at Saskia, noting the tension in her shoulders and tell-tale shimmer in her eyes and a bolt of sympathy shot through him. He instantly clamped down on it. Like him she was a victim of circumstance.

Like him she had no choice but to see this through. Pity wouldn't help either of them.

'Queen, yes. But, what does that entail? Can I drive Jack to school, go shopping in the bazaar, have some kind of job?' Idris understood the subtext all too well—she wanted to know if she'd have any freedom. The sooner she understood—the sooner he accepted—that freedom as they knew it was over for both of them, the easier the rest of their lives would be.

'Saskia, you are about to become a very privileged woman. A woman with a driver, an expense account, a bodyguard. There's a gym and spa in the rooms at the palace being prepared for you, the palace stables are world renowned, you'll want for nothing. Sure, take your brother to school, shop to your heart's content but always have at least two guards and your driver with you. Try the bazaar every now and then by all means, it will make good PR, but there are some very exclusive malls, some with Dalmayan designers, who would love your patronage.'

Her lips tightened, frustration clear on her face. 'Malls. Right. That's one day a month at the most sorted. Working out, an hour a day or so. What about the rest of the time? Maya was on the Council, wasn't she? And Patron of several projects. Will I do that?'

'Maya had a degree in economics from Oxford. You dropped out of your English degree before you even took your first-year exams,' he reminded her.

'And I've been working ever since,' she retorted. 'I'm used to being busy.'

'You'll be busy,' he said silkily. 'Schools to open, dinners to attend, dignitaries to entertain, that kind of thing. You are going to need more than a day a month at the mall because you will be photographed and judged and God help you if you are found lacking. You will need to research every guest, every function, dress appropriately and make the right kind of small talk. And you will need to look like you want to be there and like you want to be with me. That's your role. That's what I expect from you as a wife. What Dalmaya needs from you as Queen. A hostess. A well-paid, professional hostess. Is that within your capabilities?'

If he hadn't been studying her so intently he would have missed the wobble of her chin, the flash of hurt in her eyes. 'A hostess. Thank you for clarifying. That's what I needed to know. If you will give me five minutes I will meet you downstairs.'

Returning to the downstairs study, Idris tried to pull his mind back to the documents in front of him, but all he could see was the look on Saskia's face as he had spoken. She had tried to look impassive, he could tell, her hands twisted and her chin tilted high. But those green eyes were as impressive as ever and they had been burning with emotion; with anger, with humiliation.

'Dammit,' he swore. He had promised himself he would never let Saskia Harper get under his skin again but in one conversation she had brought out the very worst in him, just as she had all those years ago.

She was about to become his wife and he owed her his loyalty and courtesy at the very least. If he continued to forget himself around her then this marriage was going to be a long, bleak affair. He had to do better. For the baby's sake if not his own.

The ceremony took so little time Saskia couldn't believe she was actually married. Sheikh Malik, Idris's uncle, made a speech in Arabic and then she and Idris signed the documents. That was all. Usually, Sheikh

Malik informed her, this was just the precursor to the marriage celebration, but in their case there was to be no party, no celebration. No family and friends gathered round to mark the occasion. That was fine. She didn't feel much like celebrating anyway. A speech she didn't understand, a contract she couldn't read and no ring. The stuff of daydreams. It was a good thing she didn't believe in romance.

Short as the ceremony was her head throbbed by the end of it, her feet aching in the unaccustomed heels. All Saskia wanted was to be left alone by everyone including—especially—her new husband and go straight to bed. The beaming smiles on her staff's faces and the delicious smells emanating from the kitchen suggested she was unlikely to get her way. She glanced over at Idris. The last thing she could cope with was a cosy evening *à deux* and she had sent Jack to his friend's house for the night, not wanting him to witness the short, loveless ceremony. Her mind raced with possible excuses, reasons to put the meal off and then inspiration struck; she turned to Sheikh Malik and his sweet-faced wife with her most welcoming smile.

'I know we are all still in mourning.' The words were a guilty jolt at her conscience. So few days since her friends had died, but she was so caught up in her own tragedy the bigger tragedy seemed distant somehow. 'But my kitchen staff wanted to mark the wedding and have been cooking up such a feast there is no way Idris and I will be able to manage it all. Would you join us for dinner? And you are very welcome as well,' she added to the lawyer. Idris's narrowed eyes made it clear that he understood exactly why she had extended the invitation. But he didn't gainsay her; he probably looked forward to a romantic meal as little as she did.

A white-covered table and chairs had been set up on the terrace, overlooking the sea. Jewel-coloured lanterns were strewn through the trees and plants creating a magical effect straight out of *The Arabian Nights*. Saskia stepped out onto the mosaic-tiled floor, her throat swelling as she took every carefully constructed detail in: the candles on the tables, the cushions scattered over the benches, the beautiful table decorations, the soft music floating out of hidden speakers. Her staff had gone to such an effort and if this really were her wedding night, if she had married someone she loved, then this would be the most charming, romantic dinner possible. Blinking back sudden, hot tears, she stepped over to the terrace rail and looked out at the floodlit beach below, the sea a dark shadow beyond.

'The city is that way.' She jumped as Idris spoke, unaware he had followed her. 'The mouth of the river is just there, you see? Where those lights are, that's the ships heading up to the port. Ships have been sailing up the river Kizaj for thousands of years to unload their cargoes at the harbour here and to take spices and silks back to Europe and further afield.'

Saskia turned and shivered when she realised just how close he was standing, almost within touching distance. The lanterns cast a soft jewelled glow on him, his face a mosaic of reds and greens and blues. The light made him seem younger, like the boy she had once known. The young man she had been so desperately in love with. Her heart ached, the locked-away memories flooding back as she looked into his dark eyes.

She had been so young, just eighteen. New to university, new to Oxford, she hadn't taken long to fall in with a crowd as self-assured, as gilded as she had been then; it hadn't taken long to realise she and Maya were kindred spirits. Young, beautiful, rich, indulged, confident. Looking back, she barely recognised that Saskia Harper. Did she envy her that innocence? Maybe.

Maya had already been engaged to Fayaz. Saskia, fresh from school and ripe for adventure, had been shocked that the poised girl with laughing eyes was ready to make such a commitment, but as soon as she had seen her with Fayaz she had understood; they had fitted together in a way she had never imagined fitting with anyone, fitted in a way she found herself envying. The revelation that Fayaz was Crown Prince she had taken in her stride; her exclusive boarding school had been full of royal offspring, many without a throne, the children of oligarchs and old aristocratic families.

But she hadn't been able to take Idris in her stride. He had already graduated from the Sorbonne and was doing a postgraduate year at Oxford. Older, serious, disapproving; she hadn't understood why she was so attracted to him then, naive for all her sophistication, but somehow he had got under her skin, into her very blood, with that first unsmiling nod. It hadn't been his looks—he was handsome but she had known many good-looking boys—nor his conversation—he barely spoke to her—but she had craved his approval more than anything she had ever known.

And when she had finally got it, when he had finally looked at her, into her, as if he knew her very soul, she had fallen. Hard.

It hadn't been easy. He had been so disciplined, so focussed on his future, and she had known he thought she was too flighty, too flirty, too frivolous. She had been all of the above, unapologetically so, refusing to change for anyone, wanting Idris to love her despite her flaws. She'd thought he did love her.

She'd been wrong.

It would be so easy to fall into that trap again. To believe that she could win him round. To think that behind that cool, sardonic mask there was a boy who needed saving. A boy only she could save. But if the last seven years had taught her anything it was that there were no happy endings and, in the end, the only person she could rely on was herself.

And yet she didn't step back. His eyes were so dark, like the bitterest chocolate, his skin a warm olive, his profile proud and aloof. She knew every millimetre of his face by heart. It was imprinted on hers. Trembling, Saskia raised her gaze to meet his, preparing herself to meet the old disdain, only for a fiery jolt to blaze through her whole body when, instead, she saw the old flicker of desire, a hunger she hadn't seen or felt for such a long time.

'Idris,' she whispered, raising her hand to his cheek, the rasp of his roughened skin setting every nerve in her fingertips on fire, a flame that licked its way right down to her toes with an almost painful intensity. He had always been able to ignite her with just one touch. Slowly his hand travelled up to cover hers and she closed her eyes, all her senses concentrating on his touch, only for them to fly open as his hand dropped hers and he stepped back, beyond her reach, shutters slamming down over his gaze, the desire extinguished as if it had never been.

'Sheikh Malik, Sheikha Salma,' he said, walking past her as if she weren't there, hands open, a smile on his face as he greeted his aunt and uncle as they stepped onto the terrace. Saskia took a deep trembling breath and turned, her own smile firmly in place. She could do this. What other choice did she have?

It was like being in a play, remembering her lines and her cues, ensuring she had the correct expression at all times and that her audience believed her confidence and interest to be real, even when her thoughts strayed to those brief seconds she and Idris had stood looking out over the sea. Luckily Idris's uncle and aunt were all too aware of the reasons for the hurried ceremony and worked hard to put Saskia at her ease. Sheikha Salma was a charming woman in her mid-fifties and she spent much of the meal asking Saskia about her pregnancy and plans for the baby and suggesting shops and places to visit that Saskia might like.

The conversation moved naturally on to the Sheikha's own children, all now grown up and living away from home. 'They are all so independent, not like when I was young,' she confided in Saskia. 'Adil is right here, in the army, but Aida works for a bank in London. Very clever girl. But clever won't bring me grandchildren.' She cast a longing look at Saskia's stomach. 'Farah is a teacher in Jayah but she lives in an apartment with other girls. In my day such a thing would have been completely scandalous but she just laughs and tells me I am old-fashioned.' She shook her head. 'There we are with our big house, room for sons- and daughters-in-law, for grandchildren, and it is just us rattling around.' She laughed but there was a sadness behind the laughter. 'Progress is not always such a wonderful thing.'

'I've looked after my brother, Jack, since he was two. The hardest thing to adjust to was the lack of privacy or time to myself—he wanted to talk to me even when I was in the shower! But now I can't imagine life without him. The thought of him growing up and moving on is unbearable. I hope you get some grandchildren soon but, please, you must visit the baby whenever you like.' As if on cue the baby kicked and Saskia automatically ran her hand over her bump, offering unspoken reassurance, an unspoken promise. The decisions she had made were hers alone; she would never burden the baby with guilt, never let it know that raising it, loving it were thrust upon her.

'And what about you, Sheikha Saskia? What did you do when you lived in London?'

'I was a temp,' she said. Idris and his uncle were both listening in and she forced a smile. 'Not the most high-powered career but it had variety.'

Sheikh Malik smiled back at her in response. 'There is always a need for good temps in the world.'

'That's true. I always had work.'

His wife patted Saskia's hand. 'But now motherhood will keep you busy. For the next few years at least.'

Saskia stilled. She needed to prove that she was more than just a brood mare. Prove to herself—and to Idris—that she had worth beyond that which her body gave her. 'I'm sure that's true and I know the first few months will be hard, but I would like to work as well. I have just completed the first year of a law degree, long distance, and, even though I know I won't be able to practise, I would still like to finish it and maybe find a way to use it.'

Sheikh Malik raised his eyebrows. 'You were planning to be a lawyer? You should have drawn up the contract today. Is that what you always wanted to do?'

'Not for a long time. Originally I assumed I would head into PR or something. I did a lot of temping for law firms, mainly big city firms, and it was fascinating. I would take minutes, or type up letters and think, well, I could do this.'

'I see, you wanted to work for one of the big city firms. That shows a lot of ambition.'

'They certainly pay well.' Idris leaned back in his chair, his eyes full of scorn. 'Money's a great motivator, isn't it, Saskia?'

'No. Not corporate law, although obviously that has its place, it isn't completely full of big business types thinking about a big wage packet.' Her fingers tightened on her glass as she met Idris's gaze as evenly as she possibly could. She knew full well that he had rebuilt his family fortunes back in France, restored the vineyards to produce wine that sold for more than her weekly rent. He didn't live on some kind of moral high ground—every shirt he possessed was handmade. 'I wanted to do family law. Advocate for those who can't speak for themselves. I'd still like to do that in some capacity. One day.' She raised her water glass to Idris, allowing the defiance to gleam in her eyes. She would achieve her dreams, Queen or not. She would just have to redefine what those dreams were and not let anyone, no matter how igniting his touch, stand in her way.

CHAPTER FIVE

'SASKIA? A MOMENT, PLEASE.' It was couched as a request but Idris knew that she was fully aware of what he really meant.

It was a command.

Saskia stilled, half turned away, her full body angling towards the door leading back into the villa, poised for flight. 'It's late and I am very tired. It's been a long day.' His uncle and aunt had only just left after what had been a curiously lighthearted evening in the end.

'This won't take more than a few minutes.'

She hesitated for another long moment and he tensed, relaxing as she let out a small, indignant huff. 'If it really can't wait.'

Idris nodded at the servants, still clearing the table, and at his signal they melted away, leaving the two of them alone. 'Please sit.'

'I'd rather stand.'

He gave her stomach a pointed look, but he didn't press the matter. If she chose to be uncomfortable who was he to stop her? '*Bien.* Stand.' He picked up his brandy glass and studied the liquid just covering the bottom before setting it down and transferring the same keen study to his new wife. 'Is it true what you said just now? You're studying law?'

'Yes.' Her eyes flashed as she tilted her chin defiantly. 'I'm not in the habit of lying, Idris. I just completed the first year online—and passed with honours, with the intention of transferring to a bricks and mortar university for the next two years and for my qualifying year. But plans change.'

'Yes.' He knew that all too well. It was common ground between them; enough of a common ground to build a marriage on? It was a start. 'That's why you agreed to become Maya's surrogate? To pay for your degree?'

Her face reddened. 'And to buy a house. Jack needed a proper home. *We* needed a proper home.'

It still made no sense. 'But what about your father's money?'

Saskia stared at him, incredulity sharpening her gaze. 'Come on, Idris, you know what happened to my father. Don't tell me there's not a nice little dossier on your desk right now.'

He nodded his head in acknowledgement. Of course the Dalmayan Secret Service had torn her life inside out the second the marriage had been agreed and he had spent last night reading the slender file, disbelief increasing with every word. Where was the trust fund? The parties, the boyfriends, the socialite existence? Instead all they could find on Saskia was a tiny rented flat in Wood Green, temping jobs, menial at first, better paid once she had taken some courses to improve her administrative skills. The only scandal was seven years old and lay at her father's door.

He hadn't been able to sleep last night, trying to reconcile the entitled girl he had known, the girl he had tried not to fall in love with, with this backstreet Cinderella, toiling her twenties away. 'I'm sorry to hear about your father. I know how much you loved him.'

'Sorry? Because he was a thief? Because he committed suicide? Because in the end I adored a liar and a sham. Save it. I don't need your pity, Idris.' The words and tone were dismissive but she leaned against the chair as if for support, her knuckles whitening as she clutched the chair back.

Idris's lips tightened. The coward had shot himself the second he was discovered, leaving Saskia to deal with the mess. 'He was a clever man. He *must* have left you something. I understand you have to be careful not to flaunt it but surely there's enough money for you to live…' He couldn't believe a man like Ted Harper hadn't hidden money away in offshore accounts ready for this kind of eventuality. That he would have abandoned his beloved only daughter to poverty.

But Saskia shook her head vehemently. 'He left me nothing. Nothing except shame and debts.'

'Your mother couldn't help you?'

'She was never really part of my life. They divorced when I was small. Idris, why are you dredging this up? You knew about my mother back then. Why would anything have changed?'

'I know you weren't close but surely she didn't just abandon you?'

Saskia put her hand in the small of her back and straightened, her face contorted with effort. Idris glared pointedly at her unused chair but she ignored him, leaning against the table instead. He almost admired her stubbornness. Almost. 'She didn't want any publicity that might connect her with my father. She had remarried and her celebrity yoga business relies on good press and good karma, which I apparently was very short of.'

She blew a frustrated breath. 'I mean, I don't know if I had turned up that she would actually have sent me from her gates but there was Jack…'

Yes. There was Jack. For some reason the boy was Saskia's responsibility—which now made him Idris's. Three days ago he'd had no responsibilities beyond the vineyard and his business apart from his mother's occasional dramas and bailing out his father on occasion. Now he had a kingdom, a wife, a dependent child and another on the way. It was as if he had pressed fast forward on the game of life and been catapulted five years on with no real idea how he got there.

'Where is his mother?'

'I don't know and I don't care. That woman. God, Idris, she didn't want to be a mother at all. She was my father's mistress, I didn't even know of her existence—or of Jack's—until a week after my father…a week after he died. I was still at the house then, gradually realising just what a mess he had bequeathed me, and she turned up at the door demanding her maintenance. Apparently she had only agreed to keep Jack in return for a lavish allowance. No allowance, no Jack. She just walked away and left this tiny boy behind in the hallway, as if he was an unwanted cat…'

Idris pictured the bright-faced boy running into the villa, disgust twisting his stomach at the thought of someone just abandoning their child. 'There was no one else who could help?'

'No. It was all down to me,' she snapped. 'I was—I am—the only person I can rely on. I found that out the night my father died…'

Idris stilled, an unwelcome realisation creeping over him as he added two and two together and came up with a sickeningly certain four. Her father had died seven years ago. She'd dropped out of Oxford seven years ago. He had ended their relationship seven years ago…

Ended it because she was a distraction, because he knew all too well where following your heart not your head led. The final straw had been the evening she'd shown up drunk and hysterical. He'd turned her away—and that was the last he had seen of Saskia Harper until three days ago.

But looking back he recognised that neither drunk or hysterical were typical of her. She was carefree, sure. Insouciant. Thought rules were for other people, but she wasn't the dramatic type. He swallowed, casting his mind back to the press cuttings, trying to recall the date of her father's suicide. 'The night your father died?'

Saskia whirled around, her aches evidently forgotten as she faced him, tall and defiant. 'It's such a cliché, isn't it? The worst day of your life? And you know, until that day, every day had been pretty damn good. Since then?' She shrugged, an angry, brittle movement. 'There was the day I was fired when I didn't let my boss feel me up in the photocopier room, the day I literally couldn't afford baked beans. The day I realised Jack had been going to school with holes in his shoes. The day I dragged myself to work with flu because there's no sick pay if you're a temp. The day Maya died. Yeah, there's been some competition for the worst day of my life but the day my father died still holds the crown.'

Every word dropped heavily straight into his heart. How had he not known? Not known that her gilded life had tarnished, not known that she had willingly accepted a burden far too heavy for her? Guilt flooded through him, guilt edged with anger. Anger at every person who had let her down, himself possibly included in that tally. Idris curled his hands into fists as he vowed to hunt down that particular boss and make him regret he had ever set foot in the photocopier room.

'That day,' she continued, her eyes harder than the emeralds they resembled, 'the police turned up at college to take me home. They told me that the man I idolised had shot himself. That they suspected fraud. That there was a possibility that everything I had, everything he'd lavished on me, had been bought with stolen money. I identified the body, answered questions until I couldn't speak, saw enough papers to realise that their accusations had merit and all I wanted was you to help me make sense of it all. Somehow I got myself back to Oxford, I don't remember how. But you weren't there, not at your flat, at your college, nowhere. You weren't answering your phone or texts. I bumped into Tatiana and, although her all-day party-girl shtick usually bored me, that day her offer of a drink seemed like a good one, and so did the next and the next and the one after that because I needed to somehow be numb. I got to numb, stupidly I kept drinking past numb, and somewhere along the way I hit hysterical. That's when it seemed like a good idea to try and find you again. To find comfort.' She held his gaze, proud and true like the Queen she would so shortly become. 'And you sent me away.'

There it was. Two and two did make four, after all. He held a degree in maths and business—how could he doubt it? He'd ended their relationship on the day she had lost her father, lost her entire life. Ignorance did not seem much of an excuse. If he had known why she had turned up so late, so drunk, so incoherent, then of course he would have acted differently. Been gentler. But he hadn't asked, hadn't given her the chance to tell him. She had just had her world destroyed and he had put in the final boot, stomping down on what was left of her. Shame twisted in his gut, hot and fierce.

But the truth was he would still probably have finished their relationship, not that night but soon after. She had been the ultimate distraction and his work had started to pay the price. Idris had known his path—it was straight and clear and sensible and there had been no room on it for a red-headed siren no matter how seductive her song.

He knew all too well what happened when people threw duty away for love: it tore families apart. Duty came first, always.

For once the certainty didn't feel quite as comforting as it usually did. It didn't matter; the undeniable truth was that Idris had made a success of his life thanks to his one hundred per cent dedication and commitment. He'd restored the vineyards, restored the chateau, built up a business. The Delacour name was no longer a fading star, relegated to gossip pages, but a force to be reckoned with. He had inherited the crown as a worthy heir. As a man who achieved. A man who built and restored. It was enough. It had to be enough. It was what he had.

'Why did you?' She no longer sounded angry, she sounded exhausted, and Idris glanced over at her, concerned. The baby wasn't due for six weeks and so far he'd done a terrible job of helping her to keep her stress levels down. 'I thought you loved me. You never said it, but I could have sworn I used to see it in your eyes, in your smile. Feel it in the way you touched me.'

The air around them grew thick with memories, the scent of the night-blooming jasmine permeating the terrace. Idris's grip tightened on his glass as her words sank in, as he remembered the softness of her skin, the feel of her hand in his, the way she'd shivered when he'd traced a finger along her cheek, along the curve of her waist, the swell of her breast. 'Maybe I did,' he said hoarsely. 'Maybe I was close, at least as much as I was—as I am—capable of loving anyone.'

Her eyelids fluttered at his words. 'I'm glad it wasn't all in my head.'

'Sit down, Saskia. Please,' he added and, after a quick glance at him, she slid carefully into the chair, accepting the glass of iced water he pushed over to her with a wan smile. 'You know that Fayaz was my cousin?'

If she was surprised at the change in topic she didn't show it, nodding slowly. 'Of course, your mother was his aunt.' She looked up. 'Shouldn't your mother be Queen then, instead? Or is that not allowed here?'

'It's not been done, nor has any King inherited through his mother as I am doing, but my grandfather, the Great Reformer, didn't allow little things like thousands of years of tradition to stop him.' He stopped, visions of the proud, straight-backed man flooding his thoughts. Would he be proud of the man Idris had become? Of the sacrifices he had made? 'If things had been different maybe my mother would be in Dalmaya preparing to take the throne right now, but she hasn't set foot in the country since she was nineteen. She's not welcome here.'

'She's been exiled? In this day and age?'

'Not officially, but as good as.'

'What on earth did she do?'

What hadn't she done? His mouth twisted. 'She ran away with her ski instructor when she was nineteen.'

'Okay. That doesn't sound too awful.'

She didn't understand; how could she? 'Saskia, in this country arranged marriages are still common, and education for girls over eleven still relatively new. My mother was a royal princess, a role model, and she not only lived with a man she wasn't married to but she was pictured—extensively—smoking, drinking, flirting. She modelled, did some acting. There were nude shots. She left the ski instructor for a racing driver and then, after some public scenes, she left him for my father. My father is a well-known *provocateur*, an artist, and there's no controversy he hasn't courted…their parties, their affairs, their arguments have been photographed and written about for the entirety of their marriage.' Neither cared. His father thought even noticing such things beneath him; his mother just laughed.

'Compared to an embezzling fraud they don't sound too bad to me, but I'm the first to admit my standards are pretty low. An actual parent would be nice to have.'

He barely heard her, trying to find the right words to explain. 'That night. That night you came to me, my mother had called me. My job, Saskia, my role, was to be the sensible one, to be the grown-up. It still is. There was no room for three juveniles in my family and neither of my parents had any intention of growing up.'

'What did your mother want, that night?'

He cast his mind back to that day. His mother hadn't been able to speak at first; it had taken hours to calm her down. 'There was some transgression of my father's. It wasn't uncommon, for her to call and cry at me, but this was worse than usual. It took three hours to calm her—she was hysterical, threatening to leave him, to kill herself. To do something crazy. She is quite capable of anything when she is in that mood. I couldn't ignore her, no matter how much I wanted to.'

He poured himself a little more brandy, trying to remember the emotions of that night. It was all so long ago; he had been a different person then, still a boy in so many ways. 'For the first time, academically, things were slipping. I wasn't in control and that scared me. My essay was late, my tutor concerned, my final proposal flawed, work in general not up to scratch and I knew it was because I was spending too much time with you. *Non,*' he said as she looked ready to retort. 'The fault was all mine, but I knew I had to remedy it. My future, the family expectations demanded it.

'And then you turned up and it was like watching my parents' marriage mirrored in our still fledgling relationship, seeing our possible future in their present. My mother crying, my father frustrated because he couldn't work, I could smell the alcohol on you, you made no sense…'

'I see.'

'I couldn't allow myself to be dragged into any more drama. I couldn't allow my feelings for you to develop any further, to distract me any more. I didn't know how serious things were for you, and I am truly sorry I didn't find out and help…'

'I didn't need your help. I just wanted your support.'

He couldn't, didn't answer. What was there to say? He couldn't lie and tell her that of course he would have supported her, shouldered her troubles, carried her needs and expectations along with all the others that had been thrust upon him. They'd only been dating for a few months. His mother might throw caution to the wind for the very idea of love but Idris had spent his life living with the consequences.

'I know,' he said finally. 'But it wasn't the first time, Saskia. Not the first time you turned up and demanded attention no matter what I had planned, no matter what I was doing. No, you had never been drunk before, never hysterical—but you were impulsive and wanted me to be impulsive too.' Spontaneous, she had called it when she cajoled him to miss a tutorial, take the weekend off, jump on a train and head off who knew where. He hated spontaneity, had grown up with it. What was wrong with order and a planned existence?

Saskia twisted her water glass around and around. 'Did you ever wonder where I was? Why I dropped out? Did you ever ask Maya about me?'

The honest truth was he'd been relieved. Relieved she wasn't there to distract him any more. Relieved he would no longer be tempted and could bury himself in his work. Relieved that, in the end, he hadn't allowed emotion to weaken him. 'Saskia, you knew so many people, had so many invitations—to parties, to ski resorts, to country houses. There were so many men waiting in line for you to notice them. You talked of studying abroad, of travelling. It didn't seem like you needed Oxford the way others did. I just assumed you'd flitted on to another university, another place. Maya didn't mention you to me once. I didn't ask.'

His assumptions had strengthened his resolve. If she could drop out that easily then at heart she was the party girl he had first met, not the scholar agonising over her Marlowe essay. If she could just flit away from one life then she was a butterfly like his mother, never settling. His assumptions had made it clear he had done the right thing. His assumptions had been wrong.

'She didn't know where I was. I bumped into her on Bond Street a couple of years ago but that was the first time I had seen her since I left Oxford. I didn't mean to cut ties so completely. I went home to try and salvage what I could with every intention of returning, but one week later there was Jack. And, honestly, I couldn't face people's pity—your pity—I couldn't bear the shame, for people to know how far I had fallen. From then on it was a battle. A battle to keep Jack fed and clothed and warm. Oxford was a lifetime ago.'

'You were never tempted to walk away from him?'

'We're all allowed to be weak for a moment, Idris. We're all allowed to be tempted. It's how we proceed from there that counts. But yes, there were times.' Her voice dropped and she stared into her water glass as if it held the answers. 'Times when we were hungry, times when Jack was ill. Times when it was all so bleak and so hard that I didn't know how I was going to get up the next day and start again when I wished for someone to rescue me.' Had she hoped that he would find her and make it all better—or did she know he was no knight in shining armour for all his inherited military titles?

'So when Maya found you and asked you to have the baby you said yes.' He'd judged her with such contempt when he'd seen the contract, but in the end what choice had she had? None, just as he had given her no choice over this marriage.

'Not at first. Her terms were very, very generous but they drove a hard bargain. Three months of a special diet and exercise to make sure I was healthy. Fertility drugs, which are not pleasant, believe me. Then as soon as it was confirmed I was pregnant I was flown here, to live in seclusion. Yes, it's beautiful here and I have everything I could need but I wasn't allowed to leave. No deviating from the prescribed exercise or diet. No seeing Jack's school or meeting his friends. No sight-seeing. And you know the rest. I was locked in for life. If the baby needed anything I could give then I would be legally bound to. I would never be truly free of my responsibilities. I had to weigh all that up against the benefits.'

'And it was worth it?'

She turned her hand, staring at her glossily painted nails. 'I thought so then. I can't wish the baby away but I can wish we could turn the clock back three days and avert that accident.' She sighed. 'I didn't just jump at the money. I thought about it long and hard. But Jack and I needed a real home. And he deserved to have things other kids his age had, to be able to go to clubs and swimming and on holiday. To have the adult in his life around before school and in the evenings, not spend his time in a jigsaw of breakfast clubs and childminders' and friends' houses until I got back from work. And I deserved the chance to take my degree. To try and be something more than a glossy smile and a bright manner. But it wasn't an easy choice. And if I'd known the outcome…' Her voice trailed off but he understood.

She would have chosen to remain in poverty rather than be trapped into marrying him. He couldn't blame her.

'Would you really have done it?'

He looked over at her. 'Done what?'

'Turned your back on Fayaz's baby?'

He paused, lifting up his brandy glass and examining the amber depths. 'I told myself yes, but in reality?' He shrugged. 'I hoped I would not have to make a decision either way.' He glanced at her curiously. 'How about you? What if I'd simply cancelled the contract and told you that you could leave the baby here, take Jack and go home?' Would the woman who had given up her whole life for her small brother have turned her back on her baby?

She was silent for a long time. 'I don't know either. My pride wants me to say that of course I would have gone, head held high. But in reality?' She shrugged. 'Maybe I would still be here. Probably I would still be here.' Her hand stole to her stomach. 'He or she is my responsibility. Not because a contract says so but because it's half me. I've nurtured it and loved it and looked after it. I could have handed it over to Maya gladly because I knew she wanted it so much. But how could I have walked away and left it with you when you had so much else thrust upon you?'

Idris pushed his chair back and hauled himself to his feet, suddenly exhausted mind, body and soul. He held a hand out to Saskia. She stared at it for a long moment before laying her cool hand on his, allowing him to help her up. She made to pull away once she was on her feet but he kept her hand imprisoned in his. 'Truce?'

'Truce? In what way?'

'You're right. We are married now. We have a child to raise. Two children,' he amended and her eyebrows shot up in surprise. 'Neither of us chose this but here we are. We both have things to regret from back then, but that shouldn't stop us from doing the best we can now with the cards we've been dealt. Let's make a pact.'

'A pact?'

'To respect each other. Honesty.' Idris closed his eyes and thought of his parents' marriage. About the profligacy, the constant drama. Of the extravagance. Respect and honesty seemed a good antidote to that. So it was best not to dwell on how soft her hand was under his. Or to remember the way she was back then. Fearless and so full of passion it shone out of her. Better not to remember the way she'd made him feel. Because down that path lay a madness he had no intention of ever returning to.

Respect and honesty. They were worthy goals. They were all they could possibly ever have.

CHAPTER SIX

THE MOURNING PERIOD was over at last—officially at least. Idris wasn't sure when he'd actually stop grieving although, with a sharp stab of guilt, he knew he was grieving for his lost life as much as for his lost cousin.

With the end of the mourning period came a lightening of mood throughout both the palace and the country and Idris's advisors were beginning to discuss an official Coronation date. He'd attended Fayaz's Coronation and knew what the day entailed: ceremonies, speeches, inspections of the guard, feasts; an interminably long, unbearably hot day under scrutiny for every single second. Thankfully Saskia would need to be by his side for the whole time, which meant an imminent date was impossible.

She had elected not to return to the royal palace with him after their wedding, preferring the cooler sea air to the stultifying city heat—and the truth was adjusting to his new life, to his new role was easier for him without her. The distance gave them both the opportunity to ease into this marriage, into this truce, slowly. Time to adjust to the truths unearthed on their wedding night.

Idris headed over to the villa twice a week, but there were no more confidences, no more heart-to-hearts. No moments when memories swirled around them thick with regrets, with remembered intimacies. It was best that way. Nothing had really changed; he still had a path to follow, a duty to fulfil. It was best he walked that path alone. Besides, he was still coming to terms with the knowledge that he had wronged her all those years ago. He had been so sure of himself back then. But he had lacked compassion. Lacked honour. The truth burned into him. No wonder she could barely meet his eye, ensured they were never alone.

His PR department had waited until the wedding ceremony was completed before sending out a brief press release introducing His Highness Sheikh Idris Delacour to the world as the prospective King Idris Delacour Al Osman. The press release had dwelled on his loving relationship with his grandfather and Fayaz, and his successful business empire before briefly mentioning that he was recently married and his first child would be born imminently. It wasn't a lie even if the intention was to mislead the public into thinking the marriage of greater duration than it really was.

Luckily the docile and reverential Dalmayan press didn't look for any more details. As expected the European—and especially the British, frothing with excitement at the new Queen's nationality—press were a lot more interested in the newly royal couple and had published several exposés of their student affair, digging up Saskia's father's suicide and subsequent disgrace in gleeful detail and reliving every one of his mother's scandals. But they didn't seem to suspect that the baby wasn't Idris's nor that the marriage wasn't real. As long as it stayed that way let them dig.

He pushed his laptop to one side and swivelled his chair to look out of the office window. The palace gardens were internationally renowned, an oasis in the desert interior of his coastal country. Long terraces, each planted to a different theme, led down to the extensive lawns, palms fluttering overhead, and the garden was famous for its many fountains providing a cool comfort for those who worked inside the palace walls. Further out, beyond the lawns and just out of view, were the stables, home to over one hundred thoroughbreds, many past or present racing champions. The stables had been one of his favourite places to visit during his long holidays in Dalmaya. A place where Idris and his grandfather had bonded, where he had felt as if he belonged. He hadn't had time to visit once in the month he had been back in the country.

Saskia used to ride, he remembered. She'd said all the horses were sold after her father's death and she hadn't ridden since. Maybe he should give her a horse, as a wedding gift. It would make for some nice PR photos after all…

A buzz from his personal mobile phone interrupted his thoughts and he turned back to the paperwork-laden desk to look for it, apprehension hammering through him. Not many people had that number. His chest tightened when he saw the name on the screen. Saskia. Usually she preferred to contact him through their assistants, just as he contacted her in the same distant way.

He pressed answer. 'Yes?'

'Idris?' She sounded breathless. Frightened. He pushed his chair back, jumping to his feet.

'What's happened?'

'The baby. Idris. I think it's on its way. Come quickly. I can't do this alone. Please, please come now.'

Idris didn't think he had ever moved so fast, not even thirty-two days ago when he had received the phone call from Dalmaya telling him of his cousin's death. He wasn't sure what compelled him most—the fear in Saskia's voice or the knowledge she had called him, begged him to help. Of course, there *was* no one else. First Maya and Fayaz, then Idris himself had made sure of that. Saskia had no friends, no family. She was as alone as he was. More so. He still had his parents, little though he saw them.

It usually took an hour to drive from Jayah, the capital city, to the villa but today Idris made the journey in less than forty-five minutes, his security detail barely able to keep up with his bike. He knew that his guards disliked his motorcycle, thinking it a risk, hard to guard and dangerous to ride. Idris had given up too much when he took on the throne. There was no way he was relinquishing his beloved, carefully restored vintage Triumph as well.

He got to the villa to see Saskia, her midwife and the doula, a woman trained to be her birth partner, walking towards a waiting car. He pulled the bike up to a stop and swung off it, removing his helmet as he intercepted the small group. Saskia was pale, her freckles standing out in stark relief, leaning on the two women as they escorted her to the car. Idris tucked his helmet under his arm as he reached her side. 'Are you all right?'

She nodded. 'Yes. Only when people said it hurts I didn't realise it hurts this much. Oh, no…here we go again,' and Idris could only stand there helpless while she gripped the hands holding her up, her face contorted with pain as she was reminded to '*Breathe*, Saskia, breathe.'

'Her contractions are quicker and longer than I would expect at this stage,' the midwife told him as Saskia sagged against her. 'It's imperative we get her to hospital as quickly as possible. Are you coming with us? Are you planning to attend the birth?'

Idris froze. Maya had intended to be with Saskia, he knew. Now, although she had two paid personal attendants with her and a whole team waiting for her at the hospital, she didn't have anyone on her side, anyone who chose to be there, for whom it wasn't a job. They had called a truce. Had many years of marriage ahead. But did that mean he should attend the birth? It would be one thing if Saskia and he had married for love and if the baby were really his; this felt as if he would be intruding into a world he was not meant to see.

'No,' Saskia gasped. 'Jack. He's scared. He needs…' She bit her lip as another tremor ran through her body and the midwife and doula exchanged concerned glances.

Idris jumped at the opportunity to be helpful in a way that didn't involve witnessing childbirth. '*D'accord.* Don't worry, you just get yourself to hospital. Jack and I will be absolutely fine.'

They were brave words, but as Idris watched the car pull out of the gates he realised he had barely exchanged a word with his small brother-in-law beyond asking how school was. He didn't know any children, didn't know how to interact with them. That was going to have to change with not one but two children in the royal nurseries.

There was no sign of Jack as he entered the villa. The whole house was unusually quiet and still; the airy villa had a family air, all the staff on first-name terms with Saskia and her brother. It was usually a welcome release from the formality of the palace; today it just felt empty.

Idris wandered fruitlessly through room after room before thinking to check the terrace, where he found

Jack slumped on a lounge chair, a huge umbrella providing shade from the late-morning sun. A handheld games console lay on his knee but it was switched off and his thin face had the kind of determined set to it Idris recognised as a way to hold back threatened tears. Idris perched on the lounge chair next to him. 'Hey.'

Jack barely looked over. 'Hello.'

'How's it going?'

A shrug.

Idris blew out a breath. Was there a book he could buy—*How To Communicate with Pre-teens for Dummies* maybe? He'd met Jack maybe eight times now but struggled to think what to say to the boy—especially as it was clear Jack was confused by Idris's new status in his life and more than a little wary of him. 'Saskia is on her way to the hospital now. I'm sure we'll hear as soon as there is any news.' He wasn't sure who he was trying to comfort most: Jack or himself.

'Will she die?'

Idris stared over at the small boy. 'What?'

'Saskia. Will she die? She sounded like she might. She was crying and saying it hurt.'

'That's how it is, Jack. Having a baby hurts and there's nothing you and I can do but wait. But *non*,' he said, hoping fervently that he wasn't lying to the tense child. 'She isn't going to die. She has the best doctors and midwives in the country helping her.'

'Maya died.'

'Yes, yes, she did. But that was an accident, not because she had a baby.'

'She was *supposed* to have the baby. Saskia was growing the baby for Maya. That's a secret and no one but you, me and Saskia must ever know.'

It was a big secret for the boy to keep. 'No. Do you know why it's so important?'

'Because you are the King and the baby will be the next King if it's a boy.'

'That's right. I know it seems odd but if you have any questions or worries then just come to me, any time.'

Jack nodded. 'Saskia says we are staying in Dalmaya, that we won't be going back to London.'

'Once the baby is born you'll be living in the palace at Jayah. But you'll go to the same school you're at now. Does that sound okay?'

'Will my friends be able to visit? Will there be room for me to ride my bike?'

Idris suppressed a smile as he thought of the hundreds of rooms and hundreds of acres in the palace grounds. 'Plenty of room for friends and bikes.'

'That's good. I didn't have a bike in London and the flat was too small for friends to come over. And will…?' He hesitated. 'Saskia said once the baby was born and we went home we would have our own bedrooms.'

Idris blinked. 'You didn't before?'

Jack shook his head. 'Saskia slept on the sofa only it turned into a bed and we had to share the wardrobe and things.'

For the last seven years Idris had been the only occupant of a chateau with enough bedrooms for him to choose a new one every night of the week if he chose while Saskia bunked down in the living room. His chest tightened. 'You'll definitely have your own room with plenty of space for all your things. No sharing required.'

'And will Saskia stop crying?'

Idris stilled. 'What do you mean?'

'In London she used to cry when she thought I was asleep. When things broke or there was a school trip or when my shoes got holes. When we moved here she stopped crying until Maya died. Now she cries every night. She thinks I don't hear her but I do. I don't want her to cry any more.'

'Nor do I,' Idris said softly, the weight of his responsibilities bearing down on him. It had been too easy to forget about Jack, but the boy wasn't just Saskia's charge, he was Idris's too. And, like his big sister, he had been carrying burdens that were far too heavy for him. Idris knew what it was like to be young and helpless and yet feel that the weight of the whole family rested on your shoulders. He could at least relieve Jack of his load. 'Let me worry about Saskia, okay? You worry about school and homework. Deal?'

Jack didn't move but some of the tension left his body. 'Then I guess I don't mind staying. Dan's dad is going to teach us to ride and to sail and that will be cool.'

Idris made a mental note to get Dan and his family checked out. 'We have horses and boats at the palace.'

'You do?'

'*We* do,' he corrected the boy. 'I married Saskia and that makes us family.'

'The baby too? Saskia has to be its mum now Maya isn't here to take care of it.' The big brown eyes turned their disconcertingly direct gaze on Idris. 'And you are going to be its dad.'

A *dad*. Idris stared back at the small boy as the word echoed round and round in his head. He'd known he would be the baby's father and that was fine; father was a more formal word, a more formal role. It called to mind school reports and admonishments. Guiding and helping. But a dad? A dad was a whole other being. A dad loved and played. A dad stood on the sidelines at a match and cheered. A dad held hands during first footsteps and carried small people on broad shoulders. A dad read stories and checked under the bed for monsters. He could be a father but could he be a dad? A good dad?

He was aware that Jack was waiting for a response and tried a smile. 'I suppose I am.'

'Saskia says it makes no difference, that I'm still her boy. She says that's the amazing thing about love, that it just keeps expanding to fit all the people you need it to fit. She says I'll love the baby too but I don't know. My friend Dan has a baby sister and he says she does nothing but cry and get messy and he can't play with her. I don't think that sounds like a lot of fun.'

'Babies aren't that much fun at first,' Idris agreed. 'But I think they grow on you. I don't have much experience of them myself.' He suppressed the urge to look at his phone. He'd hear if there was a call and he didn't want to worry Jack any further. 'What do you want to do? We could sit around here and worry or we could do something.'

'Like what?'

'What do you like to do?'

'Well,' Jack confided. 'In London we mostly went to museums and parks because they're free but it's a bit hot for parks and I don't know where the museums are.'

Idris's mind flew to the stables. To how he and his grandfather seemed to strengthen their bond every time they went there. 'Come on,' he said. 'Let's go to the palace and you can check out your rooms—and then we can see about your first riding lesson.'

'Saskia!'

All she wanted to do was sink into the firm, cool

pillows and float away, but Saskia forced herself to sit up and smile as Jack ran into the room. 'Hey there, my boy. Are you okay?'

'I've been to the palace and I have not one, not two, but three rooms all to myself. And a bathroom! And there's a staircase which takes me to your courtyard so I'm not far away. And Idris gave me a riding lesson and says I have a very good seat.'

Saskia blinked at the torrent of words. 'Goodness. Sounds like you've been busy.'

'Idris says I can have a horse all of my own when I show I'm ready to take care of him, if you say it's okay. It is okay, isn't it?'

She looked over Jack's head and met Idris's eyes. He was lounging against the far wall of her hospital room—a room much more luxurious than many five-star hotels could boast. He didn't look bored or strained; he looked amused. A quiver of hope ran through her. Jack needed a father figure; she was well aware of that. If Idris took a liking to him it would make such a difference to the boy's life. He'd never complained about not having the time and money to do the things his school friends took for granted but she knew their straitened, cramped existence wasn't much fun for a growing and active boy. At least money and space were no longer issues, although myriad other problems had cropped up in their place like some kind of hydra; she sorted one obstacle only to find another three in its place.

'I'm sure it is. A horse is a big responsibility though so make sure it's what you really want. Now, are you ready to meet…?' She paused. 'Well, technically he's your nephew. Do you want to be Uncle Jack or shall we go with brothers? Up to you.'

'I'm the oldest either way but I don't feel ready to

be an uncle yet,' her brother confided and Saskia suppressed a smile at the solemn note in his voice.

'How about you, Idris?' She swallowed. The marriage was about to begin in earnest; there would be no going back once Idris acknowledged the baby as his. 'Do you want to meet your son?'

He nodded, those dark eyes still fixed on her, and Saskia smiled an instruction at the nurse. 'They put him in another room so I could get some sleep,' she said. It had physically hurt her when they took him away, even though she knew he was warm and safe and looked after. She could have sat and looked at him for an eternity and never got bored. For the first time she wondered what she would have done if Maya had still been alive. Was this instant rush of utter love because she knew he was hers to love and care for or would she have felt like this anyway? Would giving him up have torn her in two? She would never have to find out but, for the first time, Saskia was easier about the choices she had made and the life that lay ahead. It might not be what she had dreamed of but her brother and son would be with her and safe. She wasn't trapped, she was lucky.

She straightened as the nurse brought the baby, bundled up in a white blanket, into the room, shaking her head when the nurse made to hand him to her, even though every fibre in her wanted to reach out and take him and never let him go. 'It's time he meets his father,' she said, her gaze fixed on Idris.

Uncertainty played over Idris's face but he pushed off the wall and allowed the nurse to settle the baby in his arms. He pushed the cloth off the baby's head and stared down at the small, wrinkled face. Saskia held her breath.

Please let him love him.

He looked up, finally, his eyes suspiciously wet. 'He looks like an Al Osman,' he said gruffly and she knew exactly what he was trying to say: *The baby looks like Fayaz.* He did; from the silky black hair to the dark eyes, the coffee-coloured skin such a contrast to her own, he was Fayaz's son through and through. She swallowed, fighting back her own tears, grief rising once again for the young parents who would never meet their perfect son. 'Yes,' she said.

'There's a look of you too.'

She almost snorted. 'Me? There's nothing of me in there, which after all I went through feels a little wrong.'

'Oh, there is, a certain expression, a tilt of the chin. He might not have inherited your red hair but I am pretty sure he's inherited your stubbornness.' He looked across, his expression soft. 'Was it very bad?'

She shot a quick glance at Jack but he didn't seem to be listening, standing close to Idris and engrossed in pulling faces at the baby. 'I've never been torn apart by wild horses but I imagine it was close.'

He grimaced. 'Lovely.'

'No. It wasn't. Maya was keen I try and do it all naturally although, believe me, nothing about that felt natural, but in the end I had no choice. It all happened very quickly, too quickly they said. I couldn't have had drugs if I had wanted.' She blew a breath out, trying to wipe away the memories of those shocking, agonising hours; she'd felt so alone despite the team of doctors, despite her personal midwife and doula. She'd needed a friend, someone she trusted to tell her it was all going to be okay. She had even wished that she hadn't sent Idris to Jack, had asked him to come with her. He might not be friendly but he was familiar. 'So, what shall we call him?'

He glanced up, surprised. 'I get a say?'

'You *are* the dad.'

Surprise and something she couldn't read flared in the dark eyes. He didn't answer for a while; when he did his voice was hoarse. 'Something that works for all of us. Something Dalmayan, French and English for a baby with all those cultures in him.'

Saskia's heart clenched at his words. By including France in there Idris had claimed the baby as his in the most natural way possible. 'That makes it easy. It's going to narrow down the choices anyway! What do you think, Jack? Any favourite names?'

Her brother frowned. 'Harry after Harry Potter?'

She nodded. That would work. 'Maybe. Idris? What do you think?'

He was looking deep into the baby's eyes. A private communion. At her words he glanced up. 'Did Maya and Fayaz have any preferences, do you know?'

'I think they mentioned Sami. It means...'

'It means *exalted*,' Idris said softly, staring down at the baby. 'A big meaning for a little person. Do you like it?'

'Yes. I really do. Do you?'

'Yes. Come along, Prince Sami Harper Delacour Al Osman, I think your mother wants you.' Carefully holding the baby, he walked slowly across the room, bending as he handed Saskia her son. Their hands met and for the first time in weeks Saskia didn't flinch away, holding his gaze, answering his smile with one of hers. He had claimed her son, accepted her brother and by doing so he had bound her to him irrevocably. For the first time that didn't feel quite so much like a prison sentence. For the first time Saskia hoped they could really be a family.

CHAPTER SEVEN

'THAT WILL BE ALL, thank you.' Saskia smiled at her assistant, breathing a sigh of relief when the diminutive brunette left the courtyard Saskia tended to use as a living-room-cum-office. It wasn't that Saskia didn't want to be busy, to be useful, but she was hoping for something more interesting than learning how to address an ambassador and the exact depth of curtsey needed when she met another Queen.

She had come to the palace straight from the hospital. A huge, sprawling, ancient monument in marble, the Al Osman seat of power felt more like some kind of gigantic temple combined with a government building than a home. High walls kept the city at bay but the palace complex was as busy as any thriving metropolis: armed guards, civil servants, advisors, gardeners, drivers, maids and cooks working and in many cases living inside the gates.

Saskia and the boys were housed at one end of the building, their rooms at the back away from the hustle and bustle of the formal governing offices and chambers. Saskia's own suite was on the first floor: a bedroom, sitting room, small but well equipped gym, study, bathroom and dressing room arranged around an internal courtyard. Her rooms were traditionally decorated with jewel-coloured mosaics and cool, marble floors, bright throws, rugs and cushions softening the effect. The bedroom and sitting room both had doors leading onto the terrace, which boasted a small infinity pool as well as shaded hammocks and seats overlooking the vast, lush gardens. Not that she could reach the gardens, not without travelling through what felt like acres of corridors and down staircases, flanked at all times by her guards and maids. It was easier to stay on her terrace and look out.

Sami had his own suite next to hers: a bedroom, nursery, bathroom and en suite accommodation for his three attendants, and Jack's rooms were on the floor above, a secret staircase connecting his playroom directly to Saskia's courtyard. She didn't know where Idris's rooms were; she hadn't been invited to see them.

Living in the palace was like being a guest in a sumptuous hotel: lovely at first but cloying after a while. For the first six weeks, still adjusting to the demands of a tiny baby and healing from the birth, it had been wonderful to have no demands made on her at all. No laundry, no meals to even plan let alone cook, no need to lift a finger or use her brain in any way. It had been the same at the villa but there the staff had been much, much smaller, the villa her domain. If she wanted to cook or bake the kitchen was hers to use or not. Here she had no idea where the kitchens were. She relayed her instructions to one of her maids, or phoned or even ordered online. Just like a hotel.

Odd how appealing her old staple of beans on toast seemed now, eaten at the kitchen counter, book in one hand, cup of tea right by the other.

'What's so funny?'

Startled, Saskia looked up. She hadn't even heard

Idris come in—but then her rooms were about as private as Piccadilly Circus, an ever-rotating crew of cleaners, florists, stylists, masseuses and aides wandering in and out seemingly at will. 'Funny?'

'You were smiling.'

Were her smiles that rare? She realised with a shock they probably were, especially when he was around. Grateful as she was for the way he seemed to have taken to the boys—and they to him—the past was still too present, too raw, especially after its exhumation on the night of the wedding. She wanted to find a way to be friends, partners, but she couldn't help being wary. She had to protect her bruised heart somehow.

'I was just thinking that only a year ago I would have been happy never to eat beans on toast ever again—and now it sounds like the most delicious meal imaginable.'

'Order it, then. There are plenty of British supermarkets around if the kitchens don't have any in stock. Which they probably don't have,' he added with a superior sneer, which was all French.

'I can't order it, Idris. That's not the point of beans on toast.'

He didn't reply, just raised a sardonic eyebrow and she shut her mouth with a snap, achingly aware of how entitled she sounded before trying again. 'It's not the beans exactly.'

'It's not? That's a relief. The palace chef has earned Michelin stars at three different establishments. If he knew you were yearning for baked beans he would walk out on me.'

'The truth is…' Saskia looked around her, at the gorgeous courtyard in which she sat. Trees shaded the shallow long pool filled with fish, plants growing with an abandon not allowed in the extensively manicured gardens, at the carved wooden benches laden with cushions, the coloured lights that came on with a tap of an app. There was even a large TV screen hidden behind a mosaic if she wanted her own secret cinema experience. 'I'm bored.'

That eyebrow again. One day she would shave it off. That would teach him. 'Bored? You've just had a baby. I thought being a new mother was meant to be tiring and hard. I didn't know there was time to be bored.'

Stay calm, Saskia.

'Most new parents don't have night nannies, day nannies and nursery maids,' she pointed out. 'They are trying to fit in never-ending piles of laundry, buying nappies and snatching sleep. My laundry is done for me, the nursery is equipped with everything Sami needs before I know he needs it, I get more sleep than I ever have before.' She blew out a frustrated breath. 'Listen to me. It's not that I'm not grateful. I got six weeks to rest up and recover and thanks to all the amazing people who have been helping me and taking care of me I actually feel fitter than before I got pregnant. I know how incredibly privileged I am.' She paused, trying to find the right words to express her frustrations.

'For the last seven years I've worked and taken care of Jack and started studying for my degree but now I'm not needed to take Jack to school or make his snack or supervise his homework or make sure he has everything he needs. And I know that I should be relieved to be freed of some of that work but I'm not made to do nothing. I can't even get on with my degree; I didn't register to study online this year because I expected to be back in London by now. And part of me wonders what the point of studying even is if I'm never going to be able to practise anyway.'

Now she had started venting she realised she couldn't stem the words if she wanted to. 'I spend my days working out, letting the stylist tell me what to order and learning about etiquette. The highlight of my day is when Jack gets back from school and I'm not alone any more. Truth is I thought I was hemmed in in that tiny flat of ours but at least I was free to walk out the door whenever I wanted...'

'You're free here.'

'If I take my maid and the guards.'

He didn't deny it. 'It's safer that way.'

'In the palace? In my home? These apartments are gorgeous but I have barely set foot outside them in three months. I need a purpose, Idris.'

'There's time.' To her surprise he walked purposefully across the room and sat on the bench by her side. It was a long, wide bench, made for reclining, it should have been plenty big enough for two, but his proximity made the bench shrink or maybe she, like Alice, had grown bigger. He was dressed in Western clothes, light linen trousers and a short white shirt. Saskia stared at his forearms, at the light smattering of dark hair on olive skin, trying not to remember how it felt when she used to slide her hands along his arms, the strength in every muscle, the way his hands would capture hers. 'We haven't even planned the Coronation yet.'

'The Coronation?' Her stomach contracted at the thought of the pomp and circumstance surrounding such a huge event. At the thought of the publicity. She'd had a tiny taste of notoriety after her father's death; there was nothing like a former society girl brought low to get the paparazzi salivating, and she had no desire to ever be in the spotlight again.

'Normally they hold the official Coronation for the

new monarch directly after the mourning period has finished for the old; it's meant to be a sign of hope after the darkness of grief, but, for several reasons, it was decided to wait for six months this time.'

'What reasons?'

'To give you time to recover from the birth. To give me time to get my business affairs in order. To give Dalmaya time to adjust to me and for me to adjust to living as a King. So if I decided to step aside and let one of my cousins take over—or if they wished to ask me to step aside—then it could be done with as little scandal as possible.'

Of course, this was as big an adjustment for him as it was for her. She forgot that sometimes. Not that he showed it in any way. 'I didn't know you were considering not staying on as King.'

She looked up at him but his gaze was hooded, his eyes giving nothing away. It was frustrating how hard he was to read. 'I hadn't intended to. I always loved being here, thanks to Grandfather, but Dalmaya isn't my home. I'm too Western, too French. He held up his hand, turning it from palm to back as he stared at it. She followed his gaze, her own lingering on the strong, well-shaped hand, the long, elegant fingers, her pulse speeding up. 'Of course in France I was always too dark, too Eastern. Growing up I didn't really fit in anywhere. But I made myself as French as I could be. I restored the chateau, restored the vineyards. Made myself a success. Now I have to start again. Remake myself again.'

'So why don't you go back?' She wanted to add, *Why force me into this marriage?* but managed to stop the words escaping. She didn't want him to revert behind the polite screen again.

'If it was just me then maybe. But Fayaz trusted me to do what was right for his son…'

Despite herself, despite every promise she'd made to herself not to allow herself to feel anything but mild amiability towards Idris, Saskia's heart ached at the desolate tone in his voice.

'So the Coronation is in two months? What does it entail?'

'A day of ceremonies, parades, photos and feasts. I would like you to be involved in helping plan it, especially where the children are concerned. I would like them both, Jack too, to wear traditional dress. After all, he is your family and that makes him mine.'

'Jack? Why does he have to be involved?' Panic rose in her, inexhaustible and painful.

Idris's brow crinkled in puzzlement. 'I thought he would like to be included.'

'But it's public, right? The ceremony. He'll be the focus of attention. People will want to know who he is and why he's there.' Saskia jumped to her feet and began to pace, agitation twisting inside. 'His mother left him because she was no longer being paid to care for him, Idris. And every day for a month, two months, many weeks after that day, I prayed that she would be sorry and she would return for him. And then every day since I've prayed she wouldn't. Because she just *left* him with me, Idris. I have no actual legal guardianship. It didn't occur to me at first that I might need to, and then I couldn't afford it.' She swallowed. 'And I was afraid that if I tried to make him mine, if the authorities realised, then they might think a one-bedroom flat and a sister who worked forty hours a week wasn't a fit environment and take him away from me. But if his mother sees me on TV or in a magazine and realises

Jack is still with me and I have money, or access to it, then she'll be back, I know it.'

'You love him?'

'Of course I love him! I've raised him. He's mine.'

She was a lioness, fierce in her defence of her cub, and Idris couldn't help being a little envious of Jack, that the boy had someone who would always fight for him, always put him first.

He pulled out his phone and punched in a quick message then sat back and watched her pace. Saskia hadn't lied when she said she was in great shape; she might have railed against her recent seclusion but her skin glowed, her hair shone and she looked fit and toned with new, enticing curves. Curves he couldn't drag his eyes away from despite himself. 'It's usual for the King to take a tour of the country after the Coronation, an opportunity to meet all the different types of people who live here from the fishermen to the nomads, and for them to meet him,' he said as if she weren't still stalking up and down, despair flaring in her green eyes.

She halted and swivelled. 'What?'

'A grand tour. I know, it sounds a little medieval and obsolete when even the nomads have smartphones but it's the custom. Only we're going to go on our tour before the Coronation. The Council think it will help ease any fears about my dual nationality—and to be honest I barely know Dalmaya at all, only this palace and the city and the coastline where you were staying. My grandfather always vacationed there. It's important I understand the land a little more before I am formally crowned. We leave on the first leg in a week. My aide has sent yours a list of what you'll need. Your stylist is already working on your wardrobe and your assistant will make sure you're fully briefed.'

'You want me to embark on a grand tour? Are you insane?'

'Not that I know of. I thought,' he added silkily, 'that you were bored. You needed a purpose. Here's your chance. Time to practise being a Queen, Sheikha Saskia.'

'But…but…the boys need me. The last couple of months have been a huge adjustment for Jack and Sami can't even sit up yet. How can I just take off for weeks at a time?'

'No taking off needed. At least not much,' he amended. 'Unlike my ancestors we have access to cars and planes and helicopters. We may need to be away for a night or two here and there but mostly we can fit each visit in in a day. It will mean early starts and late nights but you said yourself you're well rested and raring to go.'

'A few nights? Will we have our own rooms during those nights?'

He stilled. Nobody at the palace thought it odd that Saskia was housed so far away from his own quarters. Fayaz and Maya had shared a suite but his grandfather had always had separate rooms from his grandmother and *his* father had had several wives, each with their own distinct quarters.

On the tour Saskia and he would be visiting and staying in places far more humble than the palace and in this day, this age, people would expect their French King-to-be and his English wife to sleep in the same room.

His throat tightened. He had told her that her honour was safe with him and the implication had been clear—

separate rooms, separate beds. He hadn't fully realised the implications for either of them.

The thought of housing a discreet mistress somewhere chilled him. As for Saskia, did he really expect her to opt for a life of chastity? As Queen, the standards expected of her rightly or wrongly were higher, harder, the judgements harsher. The people would turn a blind eye to any extracurricular activity Idris might choose to indulge in. Saskia would be disgraced for ever.

A sudden pain in his palms surprised him and he glanced at his hands; he hadn't realised that his hands had curled into fists until his fingernails dug into his palms. He didn't want her turning elsewhere, to somebody else. 'I don't know any of the details yet.'

'But…' She paused, lips compressed, as his aide bustled in, two folders in his arms. He passed them to Idris with a bow, then bowed towards Saskia before backing away. Saskia eyed the folders. 'What're they?'

'Answers. To some of your questions at least.' He put the blue folder down on the bench beside him and held out the green one. 'Here.'

Cautiously she took it, flicking it open. 'What's this? I don't understand.'

'The palace needs to be aware of any possible problems, Saskia. They've been monitoring my mother from the day she eloped. They've probably monitored me as well, although no one will give me a straight answer about that. And now you bring a new family into the mix and it's a complicated one. Your father left a trail of headlines. Well, we can counter that with the fact you've spent the last seven years living quietly and working hard. But your mother? Jack's mother? Jack's existence? They're more problematic.'

'So you tracked them down? I could have told you

where my mother was.' She dropped the green folder contemptuously onto his knee but her eyes flickered to the blue folder and he knew she wanted—needed—to see the contents. 'She runs a yoga retreat in New Mexico, along with her third husband. She says she has achieved inner peace. That was why she didn't want me to come over when it all happened. Too much negative energy surrounded me apparently.' She was going for scathing, pretending she didn't care, but the hurt in her eyes was unmistakable.

'She's no worry to us at all. Your stepfather…'

'I've never met him. He's no father to me in any way.'

Idris paused. 'Her husband,' he amended, 'has some wild ideas. He's written several books about UFO sightings and aliens amongst us but seems harmless. We won't be inviting them to the Coronation.' He looked at Saskia to see how she would take the news but she didn't as much as nod.

'Of course not. She walked out of my life when I was three and never walked back in again. She doesn't even send me a birthday card most years.'

'This is what we compiled on Jack's mother.'

Her composure crumpled, her hand shaking as she took the folder from him. 'I used to wonder what kind of woman had a child for money. Until I became that woman.'

His own words echoed back at him. He knew better now. 'The situations don't compare. Besides, you didn't raise Jack for money.'

'No,' she said hollowly. 'You know, Rosa was with my father for four years yet I didn't even know she existed. He bought her a house, made her an allowance but she didn't accompany him to functions or meet his friends. What kind of person is happy in that kind of second-rate relationship? She said she didn't mean to get pregnant but Daddy was delighted when she did. Persuaded her to have the baby, promised her he would look after her if she did. But he still didn't marry her. Didn't live with Jack, help raise him, not properly. Just visited. I didn't even know I had a brother until after my father died. I think that hurt more than anything else.'

He nodded at the file. 'Go on. Open it.'

Her hands shook as she flipped the folder open and then she hissed a long breath. He knew what she saw. The portrait. A family portrait. Rosa with her much older husband, a baby in her arms, a toddler by her side. 'She has more children?'

'She married well. Very well. That's Chuck Weissberger, multimillionaire retail King. They live in Connecticut in a riverside mansion.'

'She got her rich husband after all,' Saskia said tonelessly, still staring at the contents of the folder.

'She did. And he has no idea about Jack. He's very family orientated. If he knew she had abandoned a child that marriage would be over quicker than she could beg for forgiveness. She's not coming anywhere near Jack, Saskia. He's safe. My lawyers are petitioning for us to legally adopt him right now. Rosa signed the papers last week. I was going to get you a horse as a wedding present but I thought you might appreciate this more.'

The folder fell out of her hands, the contents spilling onto the mosaic floor. 'I…you…what did you say?'

'The adoption proceedings are going through. It does mean I will legally be Jack's father. As we are married it would have been too complicated to apply in just your name.' From a single, child-free businessman and winemaker to a married father of two and King in one step. From simple Monsieur Delacour to Sheikh Idris Delacour Al Osman, ruler of all he surveyed. The thought wasn't as terrifying as it had been several months ago.

'But how? I don't understand.'

'Rosa has signed a deposition to say you had been Jack's primary caregiver for seven years and giving up her parental rights and we have statements from Jack's old school in London, his childminder and your neighbours. The lawyers don't anticipate any problems. They obviously need to interview you—and me as well. We'll all fly back to the UK in a month for the final interviews.'

It had all seemed so simple when he'd put this in motion. The first day he had spent with Jack, the day of Sami's birth, it had been painfully apparent that mixed in with the boy's worry about Saskia, excitement about the baby and the thrill of discovering the palace and his first riding lesson, Jack had also been harbouring deep fears that a baby of her own might alter his own special relationship with the only mother he had ever really known. For seven years it had been just the two of them—now Jack found himself in a family of four. And something in the boy had struck a chord. Idris knew what it was like to be a child and unsure of your place in the world, in your family, that fear that everything and everyone could just disappear.

If there was anything Idris excelled in it was solving problems and the solution here seemed so simple. They were already a made-up family. All they needed to do was cement Jack's place. But now, looking at Saskia's white face, he couldn't help but wonder if he had overstepped. He wasn't really Saskia's husband, Jack wasn't his brother and they weren't a family. They were a glossy PR exercise.

'I thought,' he said carefully, 'that this was the right

thing to do.' Legitimising Jack's presence in her life made things easier for him, for the crown, but it was also his way of making amends for forcing her into a life she had never asked for.

Her face crumpled. 'I... Oh, Idris, thank you.' She threw her arms around his neck, his shirt clinging damply as her tears began to flow. All he could do was put his arms around her and hold her while she wept. Hold her and try not to notice how good she smelt, like night-flowering jasmine, how her body melded into his as if it belonged there, the silkiness of her hair on his cheek. Try not to remember that this was the closest he had physically been to another human being for longer than he cared to remember. Tried not to remember how she used to feel in his arms, how he had once made her gasp. How she had made him feel invincible, an intoxication he had fought and lost against over and over. All he had to do was hold on.

CHAPTER EIGHT

TEARS WERE A PRIVATE, shameful indulgence. They had been ever since her father's death, since the moment she left Idris's apartment with nowhere else to turn.

But now she'd allowed that first tear to fall. Now someone else was holding her up. Now arms were around her, a strong shoulder supporting her. Now for the first time in many, many years someone else had taken part of her burden and it undid her.

Saskia shuddered as great, racking sobs forced their way out: grief for Maya and Fayaz, wistfulness for the life she had planned and would never now live, guilt at how much, how very much she loved Sami, a love she knew Maya would be grateful for and yet that somehow felt like a betrayal.

Fear for the long years ahead, Queen of a country she didn't know. Worry at being married to a man she barely knew and yet knew all too well. And now gratitude. This man she'd thought didn't know her at all had realised the dearest wish of all. Jack was hers, always. Rosa didn't want him, wouldn't take him away. And the rest of his childhood would be safe and happy and filled with security.

She was barely aware of Idris's hand on her back, moving in slow, comforting circles, of his mouth pressed into her hair telling her softly that it was okay, that it was all going to be okay. She was barely aware of the solid strength of him, of the way she fitted right into him, of his subtle sandalwood scent. Barely aware until, with a gulp, the sobs began to subside and then, then she was all too aware. Each circular caress burning hotter and hotter, the touch of his mouth branding her, every nerve firing up at the feel of his fingers. She tensed, regretting it immediately as his hand stopped its torturous caress, as he lifted his head away from hers, stepped away. The absence of his touch a physical ache.

'Feeling better?' His voice was low, hoarse. Had he felt it too? That connection? Or was he just being kind, desperate to grab his folders and escape his hysterical wife?

'No.' She wasn't sure what she was doing—although she was aware she was probably making a terrible mistake. But she also knew that she was desperately lonely. Had been for a long, long time and here in this palace, surrounded by people, in almost unimaginable luxury, with two beautiful, healthy children, she was lonelier than she had ever been before. She knew that she felt safer than she had for a long time while in his embrace. She knew that she craved human contact. Touch. Idris's touch.

She'd sworn she would never be vulnerable again. Not in front of Idris, not in front of any other human. Sworn she would never let him reject her again. But looking at the suppressed need in his dark eyes, she was certain that he wouldn't reject her. Certain that he craved her touch as much as she craved his.

'No? I'll call your maid. Maybe a massage and a nap will help.' He took a step away but Saskia caught his hand as he turned, her fingers sliding into his so easily it was as if they were meant to be there.

'I don't want a massage. Or at least,' she amended, 'not from my maid.'

'You don't...' With primal satisfaction she noted his eyes flare as he took in her meaning. 'What *do* you want, then?'

'We're married, Idris. We have two children. You want me to accompany you on this grand tour, stand beside you at your Coronation.'

'Our Coronation,' he said huskily, his eyes fixed on hers.

She moved a little closer. 'Yes.'

'You didn't answer, Saskia. What do you want?'

'I want to remember what it's like being me. Who Saskia is. Not a mother, not a consort. I want to feel like a woman again.' She lifted her gaze to his, emboldened by the passion smouldering in his dark gaze. 'It's been a long time, Idris. Help me remember.'

He didn't answer straight away and Saskia held her breath. If he rejected her again...she kept her eyes fixed on his and saw the moment the flames burst into life, a bare second before his fingers tightened around hers. 'Are you sure?'

'Stop asking me stupid questions and kiss me already,' she retorted with a smile, but he didn't return the smile, just stared at her consideringly, an intense look in which she felt as if the clothes had already been stripped from her body and that she were laid bare before him.

'*Non*, not yet.'

Rejection slammed into her, hard and painful and all-consuming, but before she could turn away he had pulled her in close. 'I thought you wanted a massage.'

She froze, need pulling at her. Devouring from the inside out. 'I...'

Now he smiled, slow and triumphant. 'I asked you if you wanted a massage, Saskia, and you said—correct me if I get the words wrong—you said *not from my maid.* From which I deduce that you do want a massage. Am I right?'

Her mouth was so dry she could barely speak, her insides a quivering mass of want. She summoned every vestige of sass remaining. 'Are you offering?'

'Think you can handle it?'

'I'm sure I can handle a massage, Idris.' The gauntlet was well and truly thrown down and she quivered with anticipation as Idris drew a finger slowly down her cheek.

'Are you sure about that?' But he didn't give her time to answer; still holding her hand, he turned, leading her out of the courtyard and into her pretty bedroom, not hurrying, every step utterly precise. Saskia caught her breath as she caught sight of her bed, huge, perfectly made and suddenly looming larger than life. But Idris ignored the bed, leading her into her dressing room, a space bigger than the kitchen/diner/living space in her old apartment. Half the room was taken up with her dressing table and walk-in wardrobes, the other with a professional hairdresser's sink and chair—and the massage couch. She swallowed as she looked at the innocuous-looking platform, half covered with a white sheet.

Idris took one of the fresh, folded towels from the pile next to the table and carelessly laid it out over the sheet before turning back to her. 'Okay,' he said. 'Strip.'

Saskia folded her arms. 'Turn your back.'

His eyes gleamed. 'I don't think so.'

She hoped he didn't see her hands shaking as she

raised them to the first button on her dress. Slowly she undid it then stilled as she reached the second. She couldn't do this, couldn't undress in front of him, not while he stood waiting, watching.

'Changed your mind?' he asked softly.

Tilting her chin, she undid the second button. 'No.' Then the third, then the fourth. She wore a yellow silk maxi dress, which buttoned up the front from the waist to her throat, and as she reached the fifth button and the fabric fell away to reveal the silk of her bra, the flesh spilling out over the cups, desire washed over his face, Idris's eyes flaring. And then she understood, then she knew. She had all the control here. She kept her gaze on his as she slowly, deliberately unfastened the last buttons then shrugged the straps off her shoulders and let the dress crumple, falling in folds at her feet.

She stepped out of it, reaching behind her, not allowing her gaze to falter as she unhooked her bra and, clad only in her bikini pants, strolled slowly over to the table. She knew his gaze was fastened on her, knew his breath was coming faster as she straddled the table, slowly lowering onto it, her head cushioned on her arms, her back and legs bare to him, just the wisp of peach silk barely covering the curve of her bottom.

She had no idea how she managed to lie so still, so nonchalant, eyes closed. She heard footsteps as he crossed over to the shelf where her oils were kept, then the fragrance of her favourite jasmine, bergamot and rose blend wafted through the room. She swallowed, her insides quivering as his steps slowly but surely neared the table, the silence as he reached her side almost too much to bear. She waited for four or five excruciating, timeless seconds before he touched her, a light line drawn from her neck to the base of her spine and, despite her best endeavours to stay cool, she shivered at his touch, His laugh was low and triumphant as she reacted. Another line tracing back along the first before his hands moved to her shoulders and he began to knead.

A massage was supposed to relax and unknot, but every inch he touched tensed up with need, her skin burning under his clever fingers. Saskia buried her head deeper in her arm to try and stifle the moans his touch elicited. He touched nowhere her masseuse wouldn't touch, his movements precise and measured; all her senses were concentrated on his every move until she knew she couldn't play this game any longer. She turned and sat up, winding her arms around his neck, pulling him in, pulling him close, hungry for his kiss, hungry for his touch, hungry for him. And with a guttural moan he obliged, picking her up, his mouth on hers and carrying her through to the bedroom. Saskia knew there were one hundred reasons why this was a bad idea, one hundred reasons why she needed to safeguard her heart; recklessly she pushed them all to one side because right here, right now, this was all that mattered. She needed to feel, she needed to not be alone, she needed to be wanted, to be noticed, and under his mouth and hands she finally came alive.

Idris disembarked from the helicopter, scanning the desert until he saw Saskia standing under a canvas shelter on one side of the palm-tree-fringed, sandy landing strip. It was as if they were in the middle of nowhere.

It was noticeably hotter out here. Although Jayah was twenty miles inland it was built on either side of the wide tidal River Kizaj and so, although it didn't benefit from the sea breezes that kept much of the coast at a bearable temperature, it was usually manageable except during the very height of summer. The heat in the desert was more oppressive, a visible shimmering wall, and Idris was glad he had opted for the coolness of traditional robes, a headdress protecting his head and eyes from the sun's glare. Saskia was also traditionally dressed in long, loose gold trousers in a light fabric, over which she wore a long-sleeved cream and gold tunic, a matching scarf wrapped around her head. Her maid stood by, a bag filled with water, moist towels and suncream at her feet. While preparing for the trip there had been some concern over Saskia's fitness to cope in the desert, her red hair and pale skin designed for the cold, sun-starved, northern European climate, not the relentless sun. But she would have to endure if she was to be accepted.

She didn't ask for this, his conscience whispered, but he pushed it to one side. Neither of them had asked for it but here they were. They had to deal as best they could.

He moved to her side and their guards and attendants fell in behind them as, on cue, a group of people on horseback emerged from behind the trees and dismounted. A middle-aged man in bright robes strode towards them and bowed his head. The nomads were a proud people who traditionally recognised neither borders nor rulers, although pragmatically accepted the Dalmaya's sovereign rule. Idris and Saskia nodded in response, a polite acceptance of his role as leader of his tribe.

'*Mahajan*, Your Highness Sheikh Idris Delacour Al Osman, Princess Saskia,' he said.

Idris knew the tribal leader had studied in France and England and spoke both languages perfectly. '*Salam*,

Badr Al Bedi. Thank you and your people for offering us your hospitality,' he replied.

'Come, we have horses for you. Let us ride and talk as we go. We have much to discuss.'

'It is an honour to be asked to ride your fine horses. The mounts of the Al Bedis are coveted across the world,' Saskia said, and by the beaming smile she received in response Idris knew she couldn't have said anything better.

Two hours later he was even more impressed. Saskia had obviously read all the briefing documents and managed to keep up in the general conversation. Old topics such as grazing rights, territorial disputes and minority rights were touched on and Saskia showed that she was aware of the history and disputes, with a knack of acknowledging the issues and then deftly turning the conversation to something less contentious. She would have made a good lawyer.

The Al Bedi weren't continuously on the move, often making camp for weeks or even months at a time while smaller trading parties journeyed to the bigger cities and coasts, especially during the hotter summer months. Badr Al Bedi explained that they would spend the first day riding to the large summer camp, where his own family had sheltered during the summer. Now they had reached the last days of September the camp would soon be dispersing, the feast tonight the last in that particular spot.

Tomorrow Idris and Saskia would accompany a trading party who were taking a group of horses to the nearest town. The town was two days' ride away from the camp and Idris, Saskia and their entourage would be picked up from there. The first stage of their Royal Tour would be completed.

'It's a good thing,' Idris said quietly to Saskia, 'that you're not vegetarian. We're being honoured with lamb tonight. It's a dish always served to honoured guests.'

They were just arriving at an oasis for a rest stop and water. Saskia and Idris were slightly ahead of the group, their host falling behind to check on some detail, their entourage and most of their personal guard trailing behind, although Idris knew several guards had ridden ahead and to the side of the main group. He might not be able to see them but they would have a very clear idea of where he was while keeping an eye out for any possible threat.

Saskia laughed at his words. 'Actually I did eat a mainly vegetarian diet for most of the last few years, though that was mainly for financial reasons, but that very thorough surrogate agreement was very clear that I needed to be a carnivore until Sami was weaned. I don't miss meat when I don't eat it, but I'm not going to turn down a feast cooked in my honour either.'

'I hope you feel the same way when they present you with the yogurt. It's very much an acquired taste. Of course, you can sweeten it with honey but a true warrior takes his—or her—yogurt straight.'

'I'm sure I can...oh!' Saskia broke off in alarm as her horse danced backwards. Luckily her grip hadn't been too loose on the reins and she managed, somehow, to keep her seat as the beast neighed and then reared, its front legs kicking out. 'Whoa, come on, boy.'

But Idris's own horse had also taken a step backwards and he could see quite clearly what had spooked Saskia's mount. A viper of some type must have been dozing in the shadow of the tree and been disturbed by the horse's footsteps. It was half coiled, half upright, swaying from side to side, fangs clearly exposed. Idris couldn't tell who was more scared, the snake or the horse—or who was likely to do most damage.

'Whoa!' The horse reared again and Saskia fought to stay on. Idris's heart thumped, adrenaline running through his veins as he assessed the risks. If the viper bit the horse Saskia might fall; if she managed to dismount safely then she would be directly in front of the angry snake. Could he manoeuvre his horse over and take the reins safely or would he just spook his own horse and make matters worse? He looked behind. They were further ahead than he had realised and although several horses were galloping towards them there was a real possibility they wouldn't reach the group in time.

Saskia was still hanging on, her lips white and her face pale but determined as she battled the terrified horse, the snake hissing louder, pulling itself up further, weaving closer and closer. Idris pulled his own pistol from its holster; the pistol he had baulked at wearing when it had been issued to him, and pointed it at the snake, his hand steady despite his thundering pulse. If he missed the even more terrified snake would strike. If he killed the snake then possibly both his mount and Saskia's would bolt. He checked again. It would be at least thirty seconds before the head horseman reached them and the snake was swaying in…

'Idris. Do it. I have this.' Her voice was low and tense, her grip hardening on the already panicked horse's reins.

He inhaled, concentrated—and shot. Time slowed down to an unbearable lassitude, the sound of the pistol reverberating around and around and all he could do was take his own mount in a firm hand and wait and hope and pray… The snake buckled then collapsed and

Saskia's horse, maddened beyond any control, took off, Saskia clinging grimly on.

He swore and dug his heels in, urging his own horse after her, Badr Al Bedi and several of the palace guards close behind him as they chased the terrified mount across the sands. Saskia was hunkered down low, obviously concentrating on staying on rather than trying to check her horse. 'Just hold on,' Idris muttered as he urged his horse on. 'Hold tight.'

What if something happened to her? How would he tell Jack? How would he raise Sami, made motherless twice before he was even able to speak? How would he be able to raise two boys and govern this harsh, beautiful country on his own? He might not have chosen Saskia but she was his partner now—in every way—and he didn't want to take this journey alone.

His blood thundered as her horse increased his pace. She'd only just come back into his life. He wasn't ready to lose her again. Not yet.

She was close, so close, any moment now he might be able to grab the reins and help slow her horse. But at that moment her horse tripped, twisted and, with a sickening yell that froze his blood, Saskia fell, rolled and lay crumpled in the sand.

CHAPTER NINE

'I FEEL LIKE a prize idiot.' Saskia stared down at her strapped ankle and winced. If pride came before a fall then humility was the result of one—humility along with a sprained ankle and many bruises. 'And I've ruined the whole visit. Badr is embarrassed and I can't go to the feast and…'

Idris held up a hand and Saskia stuttered to a stop, both surprised by his high-handed manner and more than a little indignant.

'You have ruined nothing. In fact, right now, several ballads are being composed about the flame-haired Queen who rides like a warrior…'

'…and who falls like a fool.' Now the adrenaline had faded away the realisation of how close she had been to something much worse than a sprained ankle and bruises shivered at the edge of her consciousness. Much better to concentrate on embarrassment than near death.

Luckily she hadn't been unconscious for long. She'd come to blearily to find herself cradled in a pair of strong arms. Cradled by Idris. Had blinked to see the fear on his face, fear that had quickly drained away, replaced by the same calm, shuttered look he habitually wore—unless he was with the boys. Or unless they were in bed.

'I didn't think self-pity was one of the signs of concussion.' Idris held up his phone so she could see the medical website he was referring to. 'But if it is we need a helicopter out here immediately. You are obviously in a bad way. I think we should get one anyway,' he said for the tenth time in the last hour.

'I'm fine. Honestly. My shoulder and leg got most of the impact. Thank goodness I remembered all my pony club training and insisted on wearing a riding hat. I know you thought I was in more danger of heat stroke than I was of falling off but this way I got to suffer two in one.' The hat had been almost suffocating and only pride—and a childhood in which the importance of wearing a riding helmet had been drilled into her—had kept it on her head. Thank goodness she had; although there was a definite tender spot on her scalp she was sure that she had got away without any serious injury. 'Idris. It's bad enough I had to ride to the camp behind you on your horse like a child. Bad enough that I've been told to eat soup and have an early night and miss everything that was organised in our honour. If I get helicoptered out of here, two days early, then people are going to think I can't hack the desert life here. That I'm not fit for this role.'

'No one who saw you handle that horse would ever say you weren't fit. The Al Badi would love to claim you as one of them. The first thing we need to do when we get back is get you a mount of your own. You are far too good a horsewoman to go without.'

Well, they did always say to get right back on a horse. As a girl she'd been fearless, the higher the jump, the wider the ditch, the better, never thinking anything of heading straight into the stable no matter the horse's temperament. Today she realised just how mortal she really was. The thought of getting back into the saddle—of allowing Jack to have another riding lesson—made her chest swell with panic and her stomach drop, fear breaking out like perspiration. But horse racing and horse breeding were national passions—and a significant part of the Dalmayan economy—and if she was to have a role and a life here then one fall couldn't stop her.

She stretched out and winced again. Idris and she had been housed in a beautiful white canvas tent, held up by two poles, the inside draped in gorgeous orange and red silk matched by the intricately woven rugs that covered the floor and the cushions heaped on the low couches and the wide bed. Intricately carved tables housed lanterns; jugs of chilled water and bowls of fruit were dotted around the interior. It was all very inviting and usually she would have been utterly charmed. As they had ridden in she had noticed that the tents all ringed a large central square, covered over with a huge canopy, a fire pit prepared in the middle and surrounded by seats. All set up for the feast and festivities. The spicy smells emanating from the cooking tents made her mouth water and her stomach rumble and the thought of bland soup failed to lift her spirits.

'Idris, I don't need you here keeping an eye on me. Go out and enjoy the lamb and the songs and the fire. It's not like I'm far away. It seems a shame that they went to such an effort and for one of us not to attend. And you said yourself that things have been tense between the crown and the Al Bedi for many years, since your grandfather's reforms. This is a good chance for you to start off in a more positive way. I'll be fine. I have soup coming, after all.' She tried to smile and, after a searching look at her, Idris nodded.

'You're right. I know Badr takes this whole accident

personally. It would be good to show him that we are not holding him to blame.'

'It's not like he planted the snake there.' She managed not to shudder when she said the word. Saskia hadn't ever had any phobias before but she was pretty sure she was going to see that particular snake in her nightmares.

'No, but the horse should have been better trained.' Idris sounded grim and she looked up.

'That was pure instinct, Idris. He was a perfect gent up to that part. In fact…' She swallowed. Along with snakes she would be quite happy never to see that particular grey stallion again. But this wasn't about her. It was about diplomacy, about a proud man, about a country. 'I would like him. As my own.'

Idris stared at her incredulously. 'Are you insane?'

Possibly. 'He was on his way to market so let's buy him. Just think how proud Badr, how proud the whole tribe will be if they see him on TV or in a magazine. Knowing he's in the royal stables. My first real contact with Dalmaya.'

'They'll never let you buy him. They'll insist he's a present.'

'If they do, then we'll accept.'

Idris stood, obviously torn between accepting that she made sense and an understandable desire not to allow any of the family near the horse again before agreeing with a curt nod. 'I'll talk to Badr. But tomorrow you ride pillion behind me again. No arguing or I will definitely call a helicopter.' And with that he was gone.

The evening passed slowly. Saskia's head throbbed, her ankle ached and every bruise was making its presence felt in its own unique way. The soup had been delicious although she really hadn't been hungry at all once she started to eat but, under the solicitous gaze of the local healer, she managed to finish the bowl and eat some of the flatbread as well. The sounds of laughter and music drifted into the tent and, lulled by the sound, she drifted into sleep.

The sound of the tent unfastening woke her and she looked up to see Idris undressing by the light of the lantern. The shadows played on his back, highlighting his slim muscles, the dips and hollows in his back, and she swallowed. He was so ridiculously attractive. How could she keep her heart safe when his nearness made her tremble, her name on his lips made her ache? When just the sight of him half naked and unaware made her forget every bruise?

She shifted and he turned, his eyes black pools in the darkness. '*Pardon*, Saskia. I didn't mean to wake you.'

'You didn't. I wake every time I turn over.'

'I think it's best that I sleep over here.' He gestured to one of the low couches and Saskia felt that old ache of rejection spread out from her chest, chilling her bones. He was willing to have sex with her but sleeping together was an intimacy too far. In the palace it kind of made sense for him to return to his own room. Maybe. But out here?

'It's very narrow,' she pointed out, trying to sound non-committal, as if she really didn't care one way or the other. Of course she shouldn't care… 'If you fall off and hurt yourself we'll both be riding pillion. It's not going to be very kingly when you show up at the trading post tucked up behind Badr, is it?'

He scowled. 'I don't want to hurt you.'

'Idris, this bed is big enough for four. But we can put a pillow down the middle if you would feel safer,' she added sweetly, and the scowl intensified as he stalked towards the bed and climbed in. Saskia held her breath. She often shared a bed with Jack, at least she had done before getting pregnant, but she hadn't slept beside another adult—beside a man—since Idris all those years ago. Here they were again.

'You're sure I'm not hurting you?'

'There's at least a metre of space between us,' she said. 'You may be overestimating your masculine powers.'

To her surprise he chuckled, low and deep. 'It's a good thing you're injured or I'd make you regret that.'

Could it be her husband was actually flirting with her? Flirting knowing that there was no way they would be having sex as a result? *Probably* no way they would be having sex. She flexed her ankle and only just managed not to yelp as a jolt of agony ran through her. No, make that definitely no way. 'Promises, promises.'

Saskia turned on her side and faced away from Idris but the drowsiness had ebbed. She was all too achingly aware of him despite the space between them; the slope in the mattress, the sound of his even breath, the scent of him. She swallowed, want racing through her hot and sudden, the throbbing of her bruises replaced by the steady thrum of her heart, the ache in her breasts, the pull deep at the base of her stomach. It was just good old lust, a biological imperative, she knew that. She'd been without a mate too long and now she had started sleeping with Idris her body was urging her on. Evolutionary science at its most basic. But thinking scientific thoughts wasn't calming her hormones; they were continuing to jump around like excited cheerleaders urging her to cuddle in closer, urging her to 'go on, reach out and touch him…' She turned over, lifting a hand then dropping it. It was late. She was supposed to be staying quiet and getting some rest.

With a huff she turned back over, wincing as she landed on a bruise, and grabbed the thin pillow, punching it to try and get some more support.

'Trouble sleeping?' Idris drawled, sounding like a man who had never suffered a restless night in his life.

'No,' she lied. 'I'm fine. It's just...' She paused. She didn't want to sound like a whiny girl and admit every bruise was making itself felt and her ankle was tight and seemed to be three times its usual size. 'I'm a soft European who needs something more than a thin bolster for a pillow,' she said instead. 'It's hard to get comfortable.'

There was a long pause and all she could hear was the frantic thump of her heart until: 'Come here, then,' and she heard the unmistakable sounds of Idris shifting across to the middle of the bed. She scooted back a few inches until she collided with the solid wall of his body, heat instantly enveloping her, a heady mixture of body warmth and those pesky hormones brightening even more at the realisation he was bare-chested. A strong, bare arm slipped around her neck, another across her stomach. 'Better?'

'Uh-huh,' she said unconvincingly even to herself.

That laugh again, low and rumbling right through her until every atom quivered. 'Still not comfortable?'

'Well...' But whatever she was about to say was lost as Idris swept aside the fall of her hair and pressed one kiss to the back of her neck.

'Does this help?'

'Maybe a little...'

'Then maybe this...' another kiss, just below her ear '...will help a little more.'

'Mmm, just a little bit.'

'And here?' This time the hollow between her neck and shoulder. She shivered and felt his amusement reverberating through her. Amusement tinged with something more dangerous. 'Of course, you are an invalid. Tell me if it gets too much.'

'I think I can cope with a little more.' Saskia arched against him as his mouth found the delicate skin behind her ear, his breath sweet and warm and, oh, so tantalising. 'In fact this is definitely making me feel better…'

'In that case…' his hand slid up her waist to graze the tender swell of her breast '…I think it's best that I carry on, don't you?'

Saskia was awake again and, judging by the jerkiness of her movements, in some discomfort. Should he have overridden her wishes and called a helicopter to whisk her back to Jayah? The moment Idris had seen her crumpled and still in the sand, that damn horse racing away from her… His pulse escalated at the too-recent memory, at the fear that had taken over as he had raced towards her. Understandable fear: he had just lost his cousin; he was responsible for Saskia's presence in the desert, for her safety; she had two children dependent on her…but there had been something else behind that mad dash, a thought he hadn't been able to banish.

I've just found you again.

Which was ridiculous. He had never lost her in the first place; he had chosen to exclude her from his life.

He sighed. It didn't matter how much he justified his actions back then. It didn't matter that he had made the right decision at the wrong time and in the wrong way, he was still shamed whenever he thought about that last night in Oxford. It said a lot, a hell of a lot, about Saskia that she didn't hold it against him, that she was willing to be not just a trophy wife in a loveless marriage but a partner, that she didn't want to spend her life shopping and living a privileged expat dream but wanted to find a role that stretched her and gave back to the country she now lived in.

She shifted again, this time letting out a small, hastily smothered cry and Idris was out of the bed in one stride, heading over to the water jug to bring a glass over to her. He moved back to the bed, sitting by her side, helping her sit up. The tent was dim in the predawn grey but he could see that her sweat-soaked hair was pressed to her scalp, that her eyes were huge and fatigued with pain.

'Here.' He passed her the glass and she accepted it with a wan smile of thanks. Idris touched a hand to her cheek and was relieved to find it cool. At least she had no fever.

'I really think…'

'No, no helicopter.' She drank again and passed the glass back to him, lowering herself against the thin bolster with a grunt. 'I just don't want to slow the caravan down too much.'

'Don't worry about that. Can I get you anything else?'

'That glass, next to the fruit bowl. It's got some kind of natural painkiller in.'

He reached out and scooped it up, nose wrinkling as he sniffed the cloudy liquid. 'Are you sure this is safe?'

'Alya, the healer here, is a qualified nurse as well as a traditional healer. It's fine. Disgusting but works miracles. Not that I enquired too closely what was in it.' She downed the contents of the glass and pulled a face. 'Ugh. Anything that tastes that nasty has to be good for me, surely.'

He half smiled, watching her as she drank. 'As predicted Badr insists on gifting you the horse, although I want it put through its paces by the best trainers at the stables before you go anywhere near it again. We can't run the risk of it throwing you again.'

'There's always a risk, Idris. Horses, cars—we know that more than anyone.' She was silent for a moment and he thought she was falling back asleep but then she turned to face him, eyes still too wide, too shadowed but her face more relaxed, the drawn expression of pain softened. 'You know, the nearest clinic is a day's ride away. Alya works between there, here and another clinic three days' ride in the other direction.'

'Hmm?'

'That's where the schools are too. She says the children do a lot of learning remotely when they're between schools and she diagnoses a lot through video calling. It's odd, isn't it? No cars and living in tents but everyone has a smartphone.'

'It's the way of the world.' Where was she going with this? It didn't sound like idle conversation. There was a spark in Saskia's eyes he hadn't seen for a long time.

'She's the only qualified midwife as well. She says most of the women give birth in special tents, attended by traditionally taught women. Mortality rates are higher than in the cities because there's no way to get them to hospital when things go wrong. Alya lost her own baby just a year ago, a miscarriage that might have been prevented if she'd got to a hospital in time...'

'It's a tragedy, I admit, but this is a nomadic tribe. Clinging onto tradition means tragedies happen. It's the price they choose to pay. Dalmaya is a big country and there are huge swathes where there is very little approaching civilisation—or at least the trappings of it.'

'That was pretty much Alya's answer. That these things happen. But if I had concussion or had broken my leg then we wouldn't have left that to fate, would we? You wanted to call a helicopter in for a sprained ankle and a few bruises!'

'I still want to call a helicopter to make sure that's all that it is.'

'If there's a helicopter for me then why not for Alya and her patients? To get people to clinic in minutes, not days, to hospital if the clinic can't manage, to transport her and the one other nurse out to patients?'

Idris couldn't answer. Money? Dalmaya was a rich country. 'Tradition, I suppose.'

'Tradition stated that girls stayed at home and didn't go to school, let alone university—and your grandfather's edicts may have worked in the cities but not out here in the desert. Luckily Alya's father indulged her and allowed her to study and now, thanks to the Internet, all Al Bedi girls are educated and any that wish to study further have the freedom to go on to college. True, most prefer to stay at home but at least they have that choice. Technology helps girls get to school. Why can't it help with medical emergencies? Beyond a video-call diagnosis, I mean. The Al Bedis contribute a lot to Dalmayan culture—the horses, the tourist camps. We should give something back. Something of value. Lifesaving medical help shouldn't be restricted to princesses by marriage.'

Slowly Idris got to his feet, looking around at the tent, now illuminated in the pinks and reds of a desert sunrise. It all looked so traditional but the bed easily pulled apart for transportation. The glasses were made in China and bought from a Swedish furniture store. The Al Bedi might seem unchanging but they knew how to incorporate what they needed from the modern world to keep their traditional life viable. Allow their girls to study and bring their expertise back to the tribe, welcome tourists and by doing so safeguard their freedoms and their lands.

His grandfather, educated at Oxford and the Sorbonne, had been full of reformist zeal. He had taken the oil money and invested it, not into a lavish lifestyle for a few, but into a new Dalmaya. Invested it into schools and hospitals and opportunities for all who wanted to take advantage of it. But like all reformists he had been iron-willed and impatient of those who didn't see his vision—and the Al Bedi had not been the only ones who had rejected his Western influences to modernise at a slower pace. Fayaz had been King for too short a time to break the coldness between the throne and the nomads. Could this idea, a flying medical service, be the thing to bring them properly onside? Badr too was new to leadership and far more conciliatory than his father had been…

And Saskia had complained of being bored. This idea of hers could solve two problems before they were even formally crowned.

He turned and looked at her, still obviously sore but lit up with enthusiasm. 'How do you know all this? About the healer…'

'Alya.'

'She was with you for what, an hour? Working for most of that. And yet you seem to know her life history!' It would usually take Idris months if not years to work up to that level of personal detail. 'And it isn't just Alya. You were incredibly well prepared when you were introduced to Badr, not just about the right way to be introduced, but you asked all the right questions, had him charmed within an hour.'

'I read the briefing documents,' she said then smiled. 'Look, I admit that when you knew me before I may have come across as a little self-absorbed.' He raised an eyebrow and she coloured but carried on. 'Of course I was. I was an only child, doted upon by a dad who gave me everything I wanted before I knew I wanted it, raised to think I was the most fascinating, desirable, interesting person in the world.'

It should have made her unbearable, yet that confidence, that utter sureness in herself had been self-fulfilling. Everyone had wanted to know her, the girls had wanted to be her friend, the boys had all wanted to sleep with her.

'It was a shock when I started temping. No one cares about a temp. They want you to be up to speed straight away and to blend in. That's it. I blundered around my first few jobs acting—thinking—like photocopying was below me—even though I had no idea how to use the machine—that I was too good to make coffee and people should be falling over themselves to help me. A few bruising encounters showed me how wrong I was. And I soon realised that to get the good jobs, I had to be the best. Be prepared, do my homework, cause as few problems as possible and solve as many as possible. Be so indispensable they want you back.'

'So that's what you did.' It wasn't a question.

'It wasn't easy but yes, I learned what the most important things were: security codes, how to work the printer, where the kettle was, how the switchboard worked. How to retain that information. How to ask the right questions. How to fit in. Turns out temp skills are very transferrable for being Crown Princess, for being

Queen.' She laughed a little self-consciously but she was right. She'd walked into this hostile tribe a stranger and a foreigner and would ride out a valued friend and ally because she'd taken the time to ask the right questions, and, more importantly, to care about the answer. Something he should have learned in all his business dealing. Maybe he had where stock and figures were concerned but not with people.

'But you wanted to change careers?'

'Well, yes. Temping was fun but turns out it was temporary.' Her smile made it clear the pun was purposeful. 'I wanted a new challenge, to be able to put down some roots. But I liked problem solving, helping. I thought I could do that as a lawyer.'

'You can do that here,' he said, aware how brusque he sounded. 'Look into an air ambulance. Look into costings and potential problems as well as benefits and write me a report—or commission one. Then we'll talk and, if it adds up the way you want it to, then I'll talk to the Council. Or you can…'

The somewhat self-deprecating smile broadened until it shone from her eyes. 'Really? I can do that? Thank you. That's amazing. Thank you, Idris.' She made to rise but fell back with an 'Oof!' as her ankle hit the floor and he stepped back, shy of her thanks.

'I'll get your maid.' He grabbed his robe and hastily threw it on, backing out of the tent before she could say another word. He didn't want or need her gratitude, not for merely giving her a purpose and not when his plan suited him just as well as it suited her. Nor did he want to dwell on how it had felt to sleep with her nestled in close, her hair soft on his chin, her body warm and yielding against his. And he definitely didn't want to think about the day ahead, Saskia sitting before him on a horse all day long, every jolt pushing their bodies together. It was going to be a very long, very hot journey and he was going to need every bit of self-control he could muster.

CHAPTER TEN

'HAPPY BIRTHDAY!'

Saskia blearily opened one eye to see a card and present practically touching her nose and, right behind the garishly wrapped gift, Jack beaming down at her.

'Morning, tiger,' she croaked, a quick glance at her watch confirming that, yes, it wasn't yet six a.m. 'Is that for me?'

'Let Saskia have her coffee first,' Idris interjected. Saskia refocussed to see him standing behind Jack, Sami in his arms. She smiled a weary thanks at him; she had only started drinking coffee again a few weeks ago but was already as addicted to her favourite wake-me-up as she had ever been.

As she struggled to a sitting position her maid put a tray on the bedside table; figs and freshly cut oranges, little cinnamon-dusted pastries and a pot of steaming coffee making an aromatic and visually appealing feast. Saskia took a fresh-smelling Sami from Idris as he poured her coffee, adding exactly the right amount of milk to it. He was already dressed, but this was the first time she had seen him upon awakening since their night in the desert. Even on the occasions when they shared a room on one of their tours he awoke, dressed and left before she stirred and although he now came to her most nights in the palace he was gone before she awoke.

She understood it, his need to separate the intimacy of sex from the intimacy of sharing a bed, but her heart still ached when she woke in an empty bed—or when she tried to fall asleep, all too aware of the empty space beside her, his scent still permeating the pillows.

'Open it, open it.' Jack thrust his present at her and, laughing at his eager face, she accepted it.

'Okay, okay.' Slowly, more to tease Jack than out of patience, she slid her finger underneath the sticky tape, her mouth opening as the paper unfolded to reveal a slim A4 book, the front cover a posed portrait of Jack and Sami. She took a deep breath as she opened it, discovering pages full of photos of both boys, some posed, many candid shots—including plenty of Jack as a toddler and small boy, several of her posing for selfies with him. 'What? How did you get these?' She glanced at Idris in shock. Most of the photos existed only on her laptop or on her email account.

'Jack knows your password. We only looked for the albums with him in there,' Idris added hurriedly.

'There are no other albums.' She mock glared at Jack. 'A hacker eh? I need to change my password. But this is lovely, so thoughtful. Thank you.' She swallowed, aware of the lump in her throat, the burning at the backs of her eyes as she flicked through page after page, memories unfurling as she looked back at the last seven years of the life she had shared with her brother. She glanced towards Idris, trying to convey her thanks. He must have thought of this gesture, noticed she only had one framed picture of Jack on her bedside table and that was years old.

'This is from Sami.' Jack held another gift towards her. 'I helped him choose it.'

'It looks intriguing.' Saskia took the bulky, heavy present with raised eyebrows, squealing as she opened it to see her favourite chocolates, wrapped cheese, oat-cakes, a packet of scones with a pot of jam and her usual brand of tea. The food in Dalmaya was fantastic but occasionally she yearned for a Wensleydale and pickle sandwich, a chocolate bar or a cup of Earl Grey tea. 'Amazing. What a clever baby.' She kissed Sami and then Jack. 'And isn't he lucky to have such a helpful big brother?'

She reached a hand out towards Idris, who had awkwardly curled his tall frame into the small nursing chair next to her bed. He had to have organised these presents, had heard her occasional wish for a 'plain cup of English tea' or her laughing promise to Jack that when they next visited London she was going to eat scones until she burst. Their eyes connected and Saskia ached with wishing that this was real, that they really were a family bound by love and the bonds of affection, not by duty and an attraction born from nostalgia.

Her eyes roamed over the familiar face, pausing at the hollows in the lean cheeks, the early-morning stubble grazing his chin, the curve of his proud mouth, the fall of the dark hair, her mouth drying out as she drank him in. Her commitment to Jack had made it near impossible to date but the truth was that although, thanks to her temping jobs, she had met plenty of men, had had plenty of invitations, she had never been tempted to accept. Idris was nothing but temptation and like Eve she fell, night after night.

'This is from me.' His voice was gruff as he handed

over a small box and Saskia's eyebrows rose in surprise as she took it.

'You didn't have to.'

'I believe...' a teasing note entered his voice '...that the correct response is thank you.'

'Thank you.' She repeated it as she bent her head to examine the small box, her heart thumping harder than ever. Her fingers felt too big, refusing to work as she carefully opened the present, folding the paper neatly and putting it to one side, aware she was delaying opening the box.

It was probably a duty gift. She had been given plenty of jewellery over the last few months, Dalmayan custom dictating that a woman's worth, a family's wealth should be reflected in the jewels she wore. Glittering ropes of emeralds and sapphires and amethysts, jingling bangles of gem-studded platinum and rose gold, elaborate headdresses and tiaras, heavy rings—she wore them on formal occasions, for feasts and celebrations and some meetings. They helped transform her from plain Saskia Harper, hard-working temp, to Sheikha Saskia DelacourAl Osman, soon to be crowned Queen of Dalmaya. She fumbled with the catch, finally opening the box. 'Oh!' A slender charm bracelet sat inside, two tiny charms already attached. Jack leaned over, pointing to one. 'That's my hand print, all shrunken down and made into gold, and that's Sami's. Do you like it?'

'Like it? I love it.' She could hardly get the words out for the lump in her throat. A year and a bit ago she would never have believed this possible. That she could be lying in such luxurious surroundings, a warm, contented baby in her arms, a healthy thriving Jack by her side and married to a man who surely must care about her even if he didn't love her. She should be happy. It was greedy to wish for more.

Saskia lifted out the bracelet and studied each tiny charm, knowledge racing through her. She didn't just wish for more, she craved it, just as she had long ago. She had craved Idris Delacour's love then and she craved it now, and, despite everything, part of her had never stopped loving him.

'Jack tells me you have a long-standing birthday tradition.' Idris's elegantly French-accented rumble broke into her thoughts and she started, sure her wishes must be written all over her face.

'Tradition? Yes.' She smiled at her small brother. 'We always spend the morning at the V&A because it's my favourite museum and then we have a picnic in Kensington Gardens, right by the fountain.'

'With bought food not a pack up,' Jack added. 'And lots of cake.'

For the first couple of years after she took Jack in Saskia hadn't celebrated her birthday. It was too much of a reminder of what she had lost. Before every birthday had been an event, a celebration orchestrated by her father. But as Jack got older he insisted they do something special and so the tradition had been born. Her favourite museum and then a little celebratory autumn picnic.

Later, as they put down tiny roots in their neighbourhood, there had been other celebrations, a glass of wine with their neighbours, dinner at Jack's friend's house, but the birthday picnic remained a staple and Saskia loved it, never wishing that she could replace it with the lavish parties her father had always thrown for her.

'I can't manage the V&A but how do you fancy a night at the villa and a picnic on the beach instead?'

Idris suggested and Saskia almost sagged against her pillows with relief at the idea. The autumn was a particularly hot one this year and even the well-ventilated marble halls of the palace felt oppressive at times. The very thought of being back by the sea, in a place where the staff were more like friends, where she felt at home, not like a pampered guest, was the most perfect gift of all.

'Don't we have a Council meeting today?'

'I'm sure you can be excused under the circumstances. I'll make your apologies.'

'Oh. Right, thank you.' Disappointment flooded through her at his calm, almost dismissive words. Of course she didn't need to be at the meeting; of course he didn't want to come to the picnic. He was making all the right gestures but that was all they were, right? And she was a fool for wanting more, for hoping for more.

'You're not coming?' Jack looked up, the disappointment on his face a mirror to that which Saskia was trying so hard not to show. 'But, Idris, you promised me a horse-riding lesson on the beach. And you said we'd play cricket. Please come, it won't be the same without you.'

The sun had begun to redden when the nanny retrieved the two tired, sandy boys to take them back to the villa for baths and bed, Jack well and truly exhausted by a day of horse riding, cricket and swimming. Saskia turned and watched the small group climb the steps to the villa, her face soft with love. 'What a fantastic day he's had. Thank you, Idris.'

'You don't need to thank me. Besides, it's your birthday. Have you had a good day?' Idris hadn't intended to accompany the family to the villa. He had so much work to do, so many meetings to attend, a day and a night off seemed unachievable. Turned out he couldn't say no to a pair of beseeching brown eyes and a small boy's flattery—nor had he escaped the flitting wistfulness on Saskia's face when he said he'd stay behind. They didn't want anything more from him than his company. It was a refreshing change in a world where his grace and favour was sought at every turn.

'A lovely day, thanks. I would have liked to have ridden but my ankle is still a little weak. Blissful to swim in the sea though. I stuck to the safety of the pool when I was pregnant but there's nothing like the wildness of salt water.' Saskia looked a little like a wild water creature herself, the red hair still damp, pinned back off her face, a turquoise sarong knotted around her waist.

'As good as the V&A?'

'Well, I do hate to miss out on my annual pretend-I'm-in-a-costume-drama trip. I only just made it last year—we moved out here just a couple of weeks later. I was a few weeks pregnant at the time, already feeling tired and queasy, so the picnic wasn't quite the treat it usually was and even the regency costumes couldn't distract me!'

Idris led her over to the picnic area, just below the villa. A gazebo had been erected to protect Saskia and Sami from the sun, colourful woven blankets and cushions laid out on the fine white sand and several of the villa's loungers brought down to the beach. Now the light was beginning to fade torches were lit and the fairy lights strewn around the gazebo's edge sprang into life. The housekeeper and houseboy were busy setting dishes out on the long low wooden table and aromatic aromas filled the evening air.

'Shokran.' Idris nodded at the beaming pair. 'We'll serve ourselves.'

'I didn't expect you to stay for dinner.' Saskia seated herself on a lounger, peering over as Idris lifted the heavy silver lids to reveal a slow-cooked lamb stew, couscous, bursting with vegetables and plump raisins and spices, flatbreads, round falafel and a platter filled with figs, peaches, grapes and melon. 'Goodness, the kitchen have done us proud. I hope they don't expect us to eat it all. I've only just digested lunch! Do you have time to help eat enough so the cook isn't offended before you head back?'

'I thought I might spend the evening here. It doesn't seem worth going back to the palace when I promised Jack more cricket tomorrow.'

Saskia stilled, her eyes fixed on him. Idris didn't meet her steady gaze, busying himself with filling her plate. She knew as well as he did that it would take him only an hour to return to the palace, that he could be back before Jack had even noticed his absence.

Idris had never stayed at the villa before. It was Saskia's territory. He had no rooms here, nowhere to run, nowhere to hide. His pulse began to beat hard and fast as he handed her the plate and poured a glass of the rich red wine, imported from his own estates. 'If that's okay,' he added, setting the wine down beside her.

'Of course, we're married, you don't need to ask my permission.' She picked up the wine, lying back against the padded back of her lounger with a contented sigh. 'When I first came here I couldn't believe it, that this view, this beauty, was to be mine for a whole year. I'm glad you kept it on. The palace is beautiful, but it doesn't feel like home, not like this place does.'

Idris poured himself a glass. 'I'm glad that you have a place in Dalmaya where you feel like home.'

'Do you have somewhere too?' Her gaze was far too penetrating. 'In the shock of all these changes it's easy to forget that this life is almost as new to you as it is for me. Do you feel at home?'

'Sometimes.' He paused, weighing his words carefully. 'Not in a place, not yet. When I take Jack riding or sailing or Sami for a walk. When we're in Council and the leaders stop bickering and listen to my suggestions. When I see the solution to a problem.' When he was holding Saskia, his mouth on hers, her body wound round his. Then he felt at home—and yet also like a trespasser, on ground he had no right to occupy.

'You miss France?'

'Not so much France as the vineyard, the chateau.' He stopped, trying to find the right words. 'I knew what was expected of me there, who I was. I'm still working that out here. My grandfather, my Dalmayan grandfather, would tell me that his blood ran in my veins, that I was an Al Osman in all but name, but I knew that to everyone else I was the French son of an immoral woman. I had to be better behaved than Fayaz, stronger, cleverer, nicer. It made no difference. They all loved him anyway. Everyone loved him. He had that gift.'

'Did you come here a lot when you were a boy?'

Idris shifted, uncomfortable with the personal turn the conversation had taken—and yet relieved to share. Now he was living in Dalmaya full time, the memories and what-might-have-beens haunted him around every corner. '*Non.* My mother, she and my grandfather didn't speak at all. But when I was eight he invited me over. Acknowledged me as one of the family. Usually I spent all the summer holidays with my *grandpère* at the chateau so I began to spend the winter and spring holidays here. Just four weeks a year.' Weeks he had both loved and loathed. Loved for the bond with the proud old man—and because this desert kingdom was in his blood, just as his grandfather claimed.

Loathed because he was always an outsider, always other. 'There was some resistance when Grandfather named me as his second heir. This is why we must always be above reproach, you and I. There is no room for error, for scandal, for gossip. I must be my grandfather's heir, not my mother's son, and you have to be the perfect Queen. It won't be easy but it's the only way.'

Saskia nodded, her face pensive. 'Does your mother miss Dalmaya? I know when the Manor was sold, it felt like part of me had been ripped away. I was raised in that house, and suddenly I was homeless. To lose a whole country must be worse.'

'She knew what she was doing,' he said, his mouth compressing into a thin line. 'Knew that if she crossed that line she could never go back and yet she jumped right across it with no thought for how it would affect me or her father.'

Saskia put her glass down. 'I am angry with my father every day. Angry because every moment of my childhood was a lie, because he abandoned me, abandoned Jack. I don't see any reason, any excuse for what he did. But, Idris, your mother is still here, still in your life. That has to count for something.'

'Oh, I know she loves me. I know she's proud of me. She is very free, very open with her affection—everyone she meets adores her.' His mouth softened as he thought about his beautiful, whimsical mother.

'It's just in her way she's as much a child as Jack and because *mon père* thinks of nothing but his art, if he decided we needed to be in Switzerland then off we went to Switzerland, no matter that we had nowhere to live, I had no school to go to. It would work out, my mother always said, details were for other people—for me—to worry about. As I grew up I realised other children didn't spend some months with money to burn and other months without a centime, that they didn't flit from town to town, country to country. That they didn't worry about paying the rent because their mother had bought a new dress or get home from school and cook dinner not knowing where their parents were. My time with my two grandfathers, here in Dalmaya, at the chateau, they were the times when time slowed, when I knew who I was.'

'They must have been two exceptional men.'

'Yes, they were.' He paused again, recoiling from the disloyalty of his thoughts. 'Yes, but they always expected so much from me. They never met but they were similar in many ways, both needing me to right the wrongs of the past, to be everything my parents weren't, to be the legacy they needed. They made sure I knew where my duty lay and how to achieve it.'

He hadn't noticed her leave her lounger, noticed her walk around to sit by his side until a cool hand covered his. 'No wonder you got so irritated when I suggested you skip a lecture to jump on a train and see where we ended up!'

Memories flooded back. 'But somehow you persuaded me and we found ourselves up in that little town, with all the thatched roofs and the castle.'

'The sun was out, so even though it was freezing we sat in the pub beer garden and shivered as we had our pints.'

'Then we walked along the road and quarrelled over

which house we would buy. You wanted all the tiny, impractical cottages…'

'And you wanted all the boring, sensible houses with no character.'

'You would love the chateau,' he told her, sliding his fingers through her hair. 'It has all the balconies and turrets and hidden rooms you could desire. My grandfather lived in a suite on the ground floor while the house crumbled. Restoring it has taken me five years—and now it's done I won't get the opportunity to enjoy it.'

'You could.' She placed a hand on his cheek, turning his face to hers. 'You chose not to. You chose to take on Dalmaya and Sami and me even though we were the last things you wanted.'

Had it been a choice? It had felt like an inescapable destiny. 'I didn't…'

'You did have a choice. No one would have blamed you for walking away. No one but you. You don't choose the easy path, Idris Delacour, and you don't make it easy for those of us who are journeying with you, but you choose the right path.'

'Even back then?' Her breath was soft on his cheek, her eyes full of a compassion that struck him to his core.

'Not the way it happened, but you're right. I didn't respect your need for privacy or your boundaries. I just jumped straight in wanting everything my own way. It's funny.' A soft, nostalgic smile curved her mouth. 'I don't recognise that Saskia but I do envy her. Her utter self-belief and confidence in her right to be heard and loved and her knowledge that she mattered. She was a little selfish and a little foolish but she wasn't all bad.'

'She took in a small child while she was reeling from her father's death. That doesn't make her selfish and foolish. That makes her someone with a huge heart.'

Saskia's eyelids fluttered shut, red staining her cheeks. 'You make it sound far more heroic than it was. I did what I had to do.'

'Maybe we're more alike than we realise.' Idris slid his hand to the back of her neck, her still-damp hair heavy on his skin. 'Maybe it's a good thing we ended up here together.'

'Maybe.' The word was a breath as she leaned in towards him. Idris lowered his head to capture her mouth with his. They had mutual goals, they had compatibility and they had this chemistry. Was it enough? Once he had thought he might be on the verge of falling in love with her and had recoiled from the idea, recoiled from the extra sacrifices love demanded. Now she was here, their lives irretrievably intertwined. And right now, right here, he wouldn't have it any other way.

CHAPTER ELEVEN

'GOOD, YOU'RE READY.' Idris strode by Saskia and paused at the door, clearly impatient to be off. 'Is there a problem? There's time to run through the briefing notes in the car.'

Tapping one expensively shod foot, Saskia remained standing by the first of five pillars that ran the length of the aptly named Gold Salon. 'No problem, but when it's taken over an hour of three people's time to get me ready I would appreciate a comment to let me know I pass muster.'

Despite the secular nature of the country many Dalmayans were still deeply religious and old traditions ran deep. Most women still covered their legs and arms as a matter of course, and in rural areas it was common to cover hair as well, although the veil was rarely seen. Saskia had adopted these traditions out of respect for her new country. It made sense to fit in with her compatriots when she was working and mixing with Dalmayans. However, tonight's reception was at the British Embassy and she knew her outfit would be under intense scrutiny. Her decision to wear silk trousers with a matching, long, close-fitting tunic instead of an evening dress would mark her as different, apart from her own compatriots, and she wasn't sure she was ready for that, to give up her old identity so completely.

At least she wasn't expected to cover her hair in the city. Her maid had styled it into a loose, gleaming chignon, the bright red locks set off by the green and gold silk of her *salwar kameez*. But the long diamond drops in her ears, the emerald and diamond headband holding her hair off her face, the matching collar covering her throat in tiny glittering gems and the heavy emerald and gold spheres ringing her wrists and fingers went far beyond any Western tastes in jewellery. Saskia wasn't sure she would ever feel comfortable wearing the value of a house in Mayfair on her body.

'Is it too much?'

Idris's eyes gleamed as he looked her over, head to toe, her body tingling in response to his deliberate scrutiny. 'You look stunning—and I am looking forward to unwrapping every inch of you later.'

Her stomach clenched at his words and the wolfish smile that accompanied them. 'Promises, promises,' she said, walking forward and taking the arm he proffered, allowing him to lead her out of the palace and to the waiting car.

He came to her every night now and although he still usually slipped away to sleep in his own rooms, occasionally, worn out by the demands of the day, he would fall asleep in her bed. Saskia loved those nights, loved curling up next to him. She had to keep reminding herself not to be too happy. Not to take any of his affection for granted. Not to consider their intimacy as anything more than two people thrust together and making the most out of a difficult situation. As anything more than lust. To remind herself that they were getting close to a real friendship and that was more than she had ever thought possible four months ago. Remind herself that there could be nothing more.

Idris had warned her, back on their wedding night. Told her that he didn't know if he was capable of love, confirmed that he had walked away from what they had shared then without a backwards glance. Only a fool would be ensnared twice.

But no matter how much she reminded herself she still would find herself sneaking looks at him during formal occasions, find herself shivering at the touch of his hand, find herself basking in his approval when he bestowed one of his rare smiles on her, find herself needing him every night.

She told herself that this was perfectly normal—after all, he was still her only confidant in the whole country, the adult she spent most of her time with—but deep down inside, she knew. She was falling in love with him again. Not with all the fire and drama of first love: a crush mixed with lust mixed with the hedonistic optimism of youth. But with a deeper, steadier, more realistic love. This wasn't just passion or a need to be liked. It wasn't about winning, about craving, about impressing. She was falling in love with the way he made time to listen to everyone at Council meetings even when they seemed interminable. She was falling in love with the man who had a framed picture of his vineyards and chateau on his desk but had walked away from his beloved business to do the right thing. She was falling in love with a shrewd negotiator and a patient diplomat. She was falling in love with the man teaching her brother to ride. The man who spent an entire hour playing peekaboo with Sami. The man who had safeguarded Jack's future. The man who made her feel that she had something to offer. The man who made her feel that she was worthwhile.

Dangerous, forbidden feelings. But try as she might she couldn't push them aside.

Idris seemed preoccupied as their car drove smoothly along the great driveway leading from the palace to the gates, barely speaking for the first few minutes. Saskia smoothed her tunic, trying to calm her nerves with deep breaths. She had been to several formal receptions over the last few weeks, she had done her research on tonight's hosts and guests but still her stomach tumbled with nerves.

'Thank you for wearing traditional dress,' Idris said abruptly and Saskia turned from her perusal of the narrow city streets.

'Of course. I probably would have even if you hadn't requested it. It seems appropriate somehow.'

'There is still an inordinate amount of interest in us, especially in the UK press. They print stories every day, all inaccurate, print photos every time we're in public...'

The air swirled and stilled. Whenever she closed her eyes it was easy to conjure up those claustrophobic few weeks after her father's death, cameras everywhere, her face on the front pages as every detail of her extravagantly funded life was laid out for people to moralise over. 'They photograph us?'

He waved an impatient hand. 'That's to be expected but what wasn't expected is the amount of interest after several months, several quiet months at that. They report that we argue about your spending, that my mother hates you and wants to be crowned Queen...'

'I've never met your mother!'

'It doesn't matter.' His eyes were weary. 'My parents were tabloid staples in their day. Your father dominated the headlines. You're the spoiled socialite brought down to earth, I'm the wine king. To them we're a match made in heaven and truth has no place in the fictions they spin. Tonight, we will be on British soil for the first time since we married. This is a good chance to make the right impression. There will be members of the press there, influential people. Let's start putting these lies and rumours to bed. I don't want Jack or Sami reading about us the way I grew up reading about my parents. I want this intrusiveness to stop. Show them you have changed, Saskia, that you are the dignified, compassionate Queen Dalmaya needs.'

Saskia's hands began to tremble and she folded them together so Idris wouldn't notice. How had she not known that these stories were circulating—and why hadn't Idris warned her before? 'I'll do my best.'

'Do better. These parties aren't fun, not for you and I, they're work. You mustn't let your guard down just because every accent is English and the people seem like friends. They're not.'

He leaned back, every inch the unapproachable King. Saskia swallowed, trying to quell the nausea swelling inside at the thought of the ordeal that awaited her. Usually she felt a little as if she was playing a part, the traditional dress and elaborate jewellery her costume, her briefing document, her lines, and it was getting easier to step into each situation and perform. Idris was right—tonight would be different. Everyone there would be watching her, scrutinising her, would think they knew all about her and suddenly she felt more like a child playing dress up than a Queen.

The British Embassy was housed in a walled palace in the old town. Armed guards manned the outer walls but the royal car was waved straight through to the inner courtyard. The building was an odd contrast of traditional Dalmayan architecture, all mosaics, courtyards and pillars, and bureaucratic efficiency. As Saskia was escorted through the courtyard and double-height hallway, with its domed ceiling and pillars standing to attention on either side of the walkway, she caught glimpses of glass-walled offices, of laptops and printers and all the other accoutrements of modern-day work life. The hallway opened into a huge receiving room, which was all luxurious charm from the fountain in the middle to the sparkling chandeliers hanging from the high ceiling, each ray of light rebounding off the diamonds she was so liberally bedecked in so she felt as if she were in a spotlight as she moved into the room.

It was already full. Men and women in evening dress stood in intimidatingly glamorous and confident groups, every single eye turned to her, assessing her. Wait staff circulated with canapés and drinks and, with a jolt, Saskia realised that nearly everyone was drinking champagne. Dalmaya wasn't a dry country but most Dalmayans didn't touch alcohol and the export duties on wine and spirits were so high that even those that did rarely partook. Idris drank wine most evenings—his own brought straight to the palace from the Delacour vineyard's cellars—but not one of the dinners she had been to had served it.

The tray was presented to her and she hesitated, glancing at Idris for guidance, but he was talking to the British Ambassador and didn't notice her dilemma. Then he reached out and took a glass without breaking off the conversation. Saskia exhaled. *In that case...* With a smile of thanks she took a glass and took a sip. The champagne was tart and refreshing, as unlike the cheap cava she had occasionally treated herself to as the diamonds on her wrists and at her throat were unlike her mass-produced high-street jewellery.

'Welcome, Your Highness, it's an honour to have you here. It's been quite a few months, motherhood, a new country and such a prominent role,' the Ambassador's wife said as she escorted Saskia away from the group. 'It must be a lot to adjust to.'

Some of Saskia's tension ebbed away at the friendly tone. It was nice to be able to speak her own language without feeling like an ignorant foreigner. She had been so busy letting Dalmaya adjust to her, get used to her, that she hadn't put any thought into her own life here. She had her boys and, now, work of sorts, looking out for communities and people who needed help and finding ways to alleviate that need, but she still had no friends. Maybe Idris was being pessimistic; this could be her chance to meet some women she clicked with. Potential friends.

She smiled. 'It is. I have a lot of help, of course, so I haven't had to do any of it on my own.'

'And His Highness Sheikh Idris must be of great help as well. After all, he's had to straddle two cultures for many years. Have you known him long?' The Ambassador's wife's eyes were bright with curiosity and, with a sinking heart, Saskia knew she would need to tread carefully. Everything she said would be remembered and repeated.

'Many years,' she answered with a polite smile. 'We met at university. I was at Oxford with his cousin's then fiancée.' They had discussed whether to keep her friendship with Maya quiet, another layer of protection for their secret, but although Saskia's stay at Oxford had been cut short she'd been well known there and there must be many pictures of Maya and her floating around.

As they toured the room Saskia's optimism ebbed even further as she conceded that Idris's caution hadn't been misplaced. Everyone wanted to meet her, but all they seemed to be interested in was finding out any gossip about her marriage or trying to get a contact at the palace. In the first, long, hot hour she didn't meet one person she could imagine having a relaxed coffee with, let alone an actual friendship, and the lonely reality of her new life hit her anew. Her feet ached, her head ached, the jewels weighing her down as she smiled and made small talk feeling more like a robot fulfilling a role than a real person.

'Rob, can I introduce you to Her Highness Princess Saskia Delacour Al Osman. Your Highness, Robert McBride runs a well-known adventure travel company specialising in Middle Eastern excursions.'

Saskia held out her hand, an automatic greeting on her lips when she caught the twinkling blue eyes of the man she was being introduced to and stopped, her first real smile of the night curving her mouth. 'Robbie? What are you doing here? I thought you were destined for accountancy! It's so good to see you. Robbie and I were at the same college at Oxford,' she explained to her hostess. 'It feels like a million years ago since we were karaoke duet champions in the union bar!'

'Saskia Harper! I mean...' he took her hand and executed a perfect sweeping bow over it '...Your Highness—or as I always remembered you, the Sandy to my Danny. I was always hopelessly devoted to you but you only had eyes for one man—and...' his gaze cut across to where Idris stood in a sea of suits '...I see you still have. You look beautiful as always, like a vision from *The Thousand and One Nights*. So what have you been up to since disappearing from Oxford? If Royal

Highnesses are allowed to make small talk with lowly subjects like myself?'

'I think I can make an exception.' Saskia took the champagne he handed to her and allowed him to usher her to a place near the spectacular fountain. 'Never mind me. I want to hear all about you and why you are organising desert adventures not spreadsheets. What on earth are you doing here?'

These events were always the same. A lot of hot air and people trying to get his approval ahead of more formal meetings. Not that Idris could blame them. He had once been on the other side, the exporter looking for good deals and favourable tariffs, the producer knowing if potential customers would just try it then they would instantly be converted to his wine, his brandy, his brand.

It would be nice though not to have to spend an entire evening never committing himself, on guard at all times. Fayaz had known what was in store for him and, from an early age, had built a small but trusted circle of friends including Maya so he could have time away from responsibilities, commitments and those attempting to take advantage of his position. Idris had always been slower to make friends and to trust people and now he had no one. Nobody except Saskia.

Had they ever really talked during those long ago lust-fuelled nights? He didn't remember much conversation. But now they talked. Now he listened to her thoughts and ideas, ran his ideas past her, trusted her advice. It was as if they had been set adrift from the rest of humanity and they might never have chosen to spend their lives cooped up in a small boat together but somehow they had made peace with their situation, realised that by cooperating they would somehow make it even if that destination was unknown and not where either of them had set out to go. Or something, his mouth twisted wryly. Overblown metaphors had never been his style.

The noise was almost overpowering. Although most people were speaking in English there were enough other languages audible enough to make the room resemble a flatter Tower of Babel. Idris himself had conducted conversations in Arabic, French and his faltering Italian as well as English. The most relaxed group seemed to be by the fountain; a younger, more fashionable group had congregated there and judging by the peals of laughter they weren't discussing trade tariffs. For one self-indulgent second he wished he were free to head over and see what was so amusing—but the truth was he had never been one of the cool crowd. Always working, always aloof. What had Saskia seen in him all those years ago? What did she see in him now? Or was she just making the best of a bad deal? She was pragmatic, especially where providing for the boys was concerned.

The laughter intensified and he looked back over at the lively group, freezing as he saw the sea-green silk, the red hair, the flashing of precious jewels identifying his wife. She stood in the middle of the group, a half-empty glass of champagne in her hand, smiling up at a tall, fair man. Recognition flared as the man turned—hadn't he been one of Saskia's acolytes in Oxford? Richard? No, Rob. Robert McBride. They used to sing together, he remembered, perform elaborate karaoke duets, which always brought the bar to a standstill, arms wrapped around each other, exchanging kisses as if they were compliments. Jealousy shot through him, cold and sharp as a shard of ice. His eyes narrowed. How much had she had to drink? Did she know everyone was watching her, judging her? Or did she simply not care? She had always loved being the centre of attention…

As he watched Rob put a hand on her arm—*on his wife's arm*, jealousy whispered—and leant in to whisper something in her ear. Idris watched her eyes widen before she blushed and laughed. Another sip of champagne.

People were watching her—of course they were. Even without the title, the jewels, the traditional dress, she lit up the room. But the soon-to-be Queen of Dalmaya shouldn't be the centre of attention in this way, shouldn't shine so brightly or so freely. It wasn't decorous.

She put her hand back on Robert McBride's arm, laughing, and Idris's chest tightened. A soon-to-be Queen certainly shouldn't be flirting, especially not in public. Had she lost her mind? His gaze dropped to her glass of champagne. How many had she had? Was she tipsy? Her eyes glittered too brightly, her smile was too wide.

A remark was addressed to him and Idris nodded and smiled, adding automatic replies when it seemed appropriate, but he couldn't drag his focus from the group. He tried to catch her eye but she didn't look in his direction once. And then Rob handed her his glass, Idris wasn't sure why, but he was rolling up his sleeves and the group was widening around him, giving him space. Saskia stepped back too, both glasses high as she backed up and then time seemed to slow down to a trickle as she seemed to trip, turning that weak ankle, and she fell backwards, still laughing, still holding those damn champagne glasses, as the liquid cascaded down her front, turning the delicate silk translucent, the dampness moulding the material to her breasts as she fell into one of the giant urns serving as plant pots. The room came to a standstill everyone turning to look, phones pulled out in a flash as one of the bracelets fell from Saskia's wrist and fell to the floor scattering precious stones like confetti.

CHAPTER TWELVE

'PLEASE COME WITH US, just for a little while.' Jack's eyes pleaded for her to say yes and Saskia's heart ached as she shook her head with as big a smile as she could muster.

'Best not. You'll enjoy the park more if there are no cameras around, you know that. Be a good boy, listen to Faye and look after Sami.' She kissed him on his unresponsive cheek, hating the disappointment on his face, then kissed the baby, deliciously wrapped up in a padded all-in-one. 'Are you sure you're okay with them both, Faye?' Lucy, the day nanny, had the day off but the nursery nurse, Faye, had been trained at one of the UK's most exclusive childcare colleges and Saskia knew the two boys would be in safe hands. Besides, two bodyguards would be trailing them at a discreet distance the whole time. 'Say hi to Peter Pan for me, Jack, okay?'

He nodded, the sullen look receding from his face. The two of them had made many trips to see the famous statue over the years and he was thrilled that they were staying within walking distance of Kensington Park.

Saskia turned to the window, uneasy until she saw them turn into the park free of any press interest. London was a cold contrast to Dalmaya, the autumn the grey, windy, drizzly variant. Grey like her mood. It was her fault she couldn't take the boys out herself, her fault they had to exit the embassy by a side door, on a constant lookout for the press. She had messed up.

It didn't matter that the fall had been an accident, that despite appearances to the contrary she hadn't been drunk. No matter that the clasp had been weak on her bracelet. What mattered was the photo. The photo that was on every gossip website and in most papers. A drunk-looking princess, laughing as she sat in a giant, priceless plant pot, a glass of champagne held aloft in both hands, their contents dripping down her so her outfit was see-through, her breasts, her underwear clearly visible, diamonds and emeralds showering from her wrists. She looked as if she were participating in some kind of drunken orgy, not tripping over her own shoes. And to Idris, appearances seemed to be everything.

Not that she had realised that at first. He had appeared at her side like a superhero, helping her get up, shrugging his jacket off so that she could slip it on, joking that it was a good idea he had worn Western clothes, taking the glasses out of her hands and putting them on a tray and then escorting her from the room, all before she had really grasped what had happened. But when she had turned to thank him in the car he had frozen her out. 'We'll talk about this later,' he had said, as if she were an errant teen, not his wife. But there had been no later. He hadn't come to her and she hadn't been invited to any Council meetings. Instead she had been left alone in her rooms—to think about what she had done?—until it was time to travel to London. She had assumed Idris would be accompanying them but he wasn't in the car nor on the private jet and there was no sight of him here in the embassy nor any indication that he was planning to join her there.

He had warned her, it was true. She had to be dignified, make sure there were no errors, and she had ignored his advice, giddy at seeing a friendly face. But the punishment outweighed the crime. Was this how it would be? Would she spend her entire marriage fitting in, treading carefully, alone? Idris had walked away before—and by his own admission he hadn't looked back even once.

She wouldn't, couldn't live like that. Couldn't set that kind of example to her boys. Couldn't undo those painful seven years of self-discovery and growth.

But Idris and she were married and tomorrow she would be talking to a social worker, proving that she was the right person to look after Jack, that Idris was the right person to father him. And he wasn't here. Even if he turned up would they be able to put on a united front? Could she spend the rest of her life pretending?

Even worse the paparazzi were everywhere. The social worker would have to be escorted through them, which was going to be an excellent start to the interview. The photo had stirred the already feverish press into a feeding frenzy and her father's suicide, Idris's mother's elopement, their own affair at Oxford were dissected, written about and discussed as if they held the answer to world peace, climate change and space travel in their sordid details. She hadn't been able to take Jack to the theatre or the museums or anything she had promised him; instead she had been stuck inside the Georgian town house that housed the embassy, just as she had been stuck inside the palace, inside the villa.

Saskia curled her hands into fists, blinking fiercely. No more tears. She was done with them. She was an adult now, not a teen forced to grow up too soon. She had two boys to care for and she needed to decide how she wanted to live the rest of her life. Was she any happier now for all her designer clothes and the diamond watch on her wrist?

If she wasn't prepared to live like this, then what were her options? She swallowed. Divorce, she supposed. Divorce wouldn't affect Sami's chance to inherit the throne. He was legitimate now, after all. And if the adoption was finalised first then Jack would be safe. And for all Idris's threats nearly six months ago she knew now he wouldn't leave the children penniless. Nor did she think he would try and take them from her.

She looked around her at the warm colours and comfortable, elegant furniture. Once she had walked the streets of Kensington, playing the *Where would I like to live?* game. She had always chosen either a mews house or a town house, complete with basement and attic like the houses in the old-fashioned children's stories she loved so much. Nothing ostentatious. No basement cinemas. Instead she had yearned for a large kitchen diner, for cosy furniture you could sit on, warm furnishings, not acres of marble covered in spindly chairs. No gilt.

Here she was in exactly that house, in a large Georgian terrace with black iron railings in the front and a garden out back. The royal apartments were situated on the first and second floors and the décor was testament to Maya's good taste, showcasing the best of Dalmayan décor while still accommodating itself to the vagaries of British weather with stoves, throws and huge rugs giving the large rooms a much-needed cosy feel. Saskia had made it, was living in her dream home. And yet her victory was completely hollow.

Despite the warmth Saskia shivered. It was time to take control of her life, not allow circumstances to buffet her from disaster to makeshift solution. Taking care of Jack, getting pregnant, marrying Idris, these had all been thrust upon her and just because two out of the three were the best things that could have happened didn't make her lack of agency any less real.

As for that third...marrying Idris had brought her security, true, financially and personally. The clothes she wore cost more than her previous entire wardrobe had, the watch on her wrist would have paid for a year's rent. Sami was hers in every way and soon Jack would be. Hopefully. But she couldn't spend her life with someone who didn't like her. The knowledge she was in love with him just made her isolation worse.

Accidents happened and there was every chance Saskia would mess up again unless she spent her life hidden in the confines of the palace walls. If Idris couldn't understand that then what chance did she have? Maya had often spoken about the future pressures awaiting her as Fayaz's wife and Queen. Society held women to a higher, more unachievable standard, she had said one night, and it was doubly, triply true in Middle Eastern countries, even ones as theoretically progressive as Dalmaya. She loved Fayaz, but she knew marrying him meant surrendering many of the freedoms she took for granted. That she would be watched, judged every moment. But, she said, with Fayaz by her side, supporting her, needing her, it would be worth it.

A dull ache pulsed in Saskia's chest, in her heart. That, right there, was the crux of the matter. Maya didn't just love Fayaz, she had known that she could depend on him too, no matter what. Could Saskia say the same of Idris? If he truly supported her, needed her, then they could laugh off any subsequent embarrassments. But if he was just going to freeze her out...

She deserved better. She was no longer a spoiled

teenager. She was a hard-working mother of two with so much love to give and if that wasn't enough for Idris…

Staring blindly out of the window at the Georgian square, at the private garden in the middle of the square, at the photographers still loitering with intent, Saskia acknowledged the truth: she couldn't live this way, loving Idris, destined to disappoint him. She couldn't raise the boys with that kind of marriage as a role model. She turned and picked up her phone, finding Idris's details, and fired off a quick text.

We need to talk. In person.

Idris's phone buzzed and he glanced at the screen to see Saskia's name flash up followed by a short text. Just four words but they shot straight to his heart. The words *We need to talk* never boded well but, he conceded, he didn't deserve anything more. He had left Saskia to travel to England alone, left her to face the fallout from the photo alone. If he had stayed next to her, laughed the picture off, then the story would have died by now but his absence was raising speculative headlines.

He got stiffly to his feet and headed over to the window, looking out over the old courtyard, at the stone barns and the grey walls. He should have followed Saskia to London; instead he had come home, to Chateau Delacour. Oh, he still needed to sign some papers, to delegate some more of the responsibilities, but he knew he could have done that from the palace or the London Embassy. The vineyard was running smoothly in his absence thanks to his more than capable manager but the chateau was his home in a way the palace could never be. Generations of Delacours had lived here and tended the fields just as generations of Al Osmans had lived in the palace and tended Dalmaya.

Maybe he could step down when Sami was old enough and return here, to vineyards and fields. To the old grey chateau, weathered and crumbling in parts. To the deep green of the French countryside and the peace and tranquillity. To a life where a mistake meant ruining a year's vintage, not ruining a country, a life, a marriage. To a place that used to feel like home.

He should have gone to London. He just didn't know how to speak to Saskia, what to say. Where to begin. He'd spent his life avoiding drama in every permutation. He didn't have the weapons to deal with it now. Or the armour.

He needed a walk, wanted to examine the bare vines. The grapes had all been picked in his absence, a few trodden in the traditional way at the harvest festival, the rest pressed. He'd missed both. Hadn't tasted the grapes, hadn't stood in the traditional wooden tub, barefooted, the grapes squelching under his cleansed feet. Despite a childhood being dragged around France, around Europe, despite the darker skin and name that marked him out as foreign in a countryside that still regarded outsiders with suspicion, he had always felt at home here. Here and in the stables at the palace. These were the places his two grandfathers, proud men who had never met, had passed down their wisdom and their traditions and their family pride. He didn't think either would be proud of him just now.

Nor should they be.

He reached the front door as a car drew up, a sleek silver convertible he didn't recognise. His chest tightened as a chic, petite figure sprang from the driver's side, her dark hair barely touched with grey swept up in a loose bun, huge sunglasses obscuring half her famously beautiful face.

'Yaa bunaaya,' she said, hands outstretched towards him.

'Maman.' It took a second for him to recover from the shock of her arrival and step forward to take her hands and kiss her on both cheeks. 'This is a surprise.'

'But a welcome one, I hope?' She reverted to the English they usually spoke at home. His father had no Arabic and, despite living most of her adult life in France, Princess Zara still spoke barely passable tourist French.

'Of course. Come on in. Would you like coffee?'

'But you were just leaving.'

'Only for a walk.'

'Then I shall accompany you and we shall dine together later. You are sure I am not interrupting you, Idris? You aren't on your way to London perhaps?'

'Tomorrow.' He couldn't miss the social worker's visit and Saskia was right. They did need to talk. 'You seem very well informed about my whereabouts.'

'A mother has her ways, even a mother who missed her son's wedding and has yet to meet her grandson?' She raised an eyebrow and shame shot through him. Shame mingled with uncertainty. Lying about Sami's heritage seemed like the right thing to do in the abstract but lying to his own parents was another thing completely. And would they tell Sami the truth one day? After all, Jack knew some version of it. The marriage, the deception had all made such sense in those first grief-laden days but now nothing seemed to make any sense at all.

He took her arm and, after shooting an incredulous glance at her delicately heeled suede boots, which seemed totally unsuited for walking through the vineyards, set off away from the house. He let her chatter on for some minutes; about his father's latest project, their plan to move to the Alps for the winter, some gossip about mutual friends before he said jerkily: 'Sami is your great-nephew, not your grandson, although I consider him my son and I hope you will think of him as a grandchild.'

'I see.' She didn't, he noted, sound surprised.

'Maya had trouble conceiving and so she asked Saskia, my wife…' if his mother noticed him stumble over the words she made no sign '…to have a child for her. As a surrogate. Fayaz was the biological father and Saskia the mother. But they died before the baby was born and before they could acknowledge him as theirs. So I…'

'So you married the mother, told the world the baby is yours so he can inherit. Of course you did. It is exactly what I would expect you to do.' Her voice was oddly neutral, neither approving or disapproving.

'What else could I do?'

His mother patted his hand. 'You could have walked away, Idris. No one would have blamed you. But you were always one to shoulder all the responsibility whether it was yours to shoulder or not. So, I have a daughter-in-law and a grandson. When will I meet them and why are you not with them?'

Her words reverberated around his head. She made it sound as if he had choices. As if he could just walk away from his duties and responsibilities—as she and his father had. Didn't she realise that someone had to pick up behind them? 'You've seen the photo, I expect. The headlines. The speculation. Is that why you're here?'

Her hand tightened on his arm. 'I need a reason to

see my son? It's not easy when you have made it clear you don't want me in Dalmaya, never mind that it was my home once. But yes, I saw the photo. Not that it matters. Photos are never the whole story, not even half the story. The press are never kind to the young and the privileged once they transgress and she, I think, is being punished more for her father's sins, for my supposed sins, than for one moment's lapse in concentration. Is she managing?'

'As far as I am aware.'

'As far as you…' Her lips compressed and she didn't speak for a long moment. They reached the edge of the vineyards, stretching out over undulating low hills, the sky a clear blue, the air crisp with the hint of an autumnal chill. The Princess tugged him towards a bench, set in the side of the vineyard, placed there for the tourists who came to watch the grapes grow, the wine made, to sample and to buy, and, after gingerly inspecting it for dirt, sat down and looked at her son.

'I blame myself, Idris. Your father, he likes me full of *joie-de-vivre* and so I am. Not thinking about tomorrow or worrying about what-ifs. He didn't want to be weighed down by responsibility, by all this…' She waved her hand, encompassing the vineyards and the chateau. 'By his name and expectations. That was a breath of fresh air to me, as someone for whom family expectations had been so all demanding.'

'So you both just turned your backs on everything and everyone.' Leaving him to fulfil both families' expectations.

'No, no. I was already disgraced, remember? Your grandfather. He had plans and we all had our place in those plans. Me? I was to be the example of perfect modern womanhood: educated and career-minded, chaste and sensible. I was to study and then come back to Dalmaya and spearhead women's education. Marry wisely and raise my children to carry on his dreams. I hated to study, Idris, and knowing I had years and years ahead of me… Running off with Pierre wasn't a moment of madness, it was calculated. A Dalmayan Princess who eloped with her ski instructor? Worse, who left him within a year? I knew I would be free. I didn't realise…' here her voice faltered '…that my freedom would be so absolute. That your grandfather, your uncle would cut me off so completely. But if I had known I would still have done exactly the same.'

Idris sat and stared over the fields as his mother's words sank in. He had always thought of her as impulsive and thoughtless. Not someone weighed down by expectations who sought her own path to freedom.

'I met your father soon afterwards. He was so talented and his ideas, his rejection of his birthright and all that went along with it called to me. It's not easy being married to a genius, especially one who thinks commercial is a dirty word. Neither he nor I were brought up to budget and I know it wasn't easy living from boom to bust over and over. Travelling around all the time. And I know that we are both so volatile, it wasn't the most peaceful of childhoods. Too much smashed crockery. That's why I made sure you spent so much time here, or in Dalmaya. I was happy that my father wanted *you* there, if not me. But maybe those two old men put too much on you. Wanted you to make up for the sins of your parents. I was so angry when my father went against convention and named you in the succession, when your *grandpère* left you this place with its debts and obligations. But you like responsibility. You have made the vineyard a success. I know you will be a great King, my son.'

'Thank you.' It was hard to get the words out.

'But you can be…' she hesitated, choosing her words carefully, it seemed '…rigid. You make your mind up and that's that. I am feckless and court scandal. Well.' She shrugged. 'I see why you think that. I don't always think first and the papers will never allow me to forget my transgressions. But I love you—I always have. I love your father. I would never do anything to endanger our family. Even when your father had that infatuation with that model of his, you remember?'

'I remember.' His mother had phoned him, hysterical. That was the day Saskia had come to him for help and, angry at already losing his day to one woman's drama, he had turned her away, turned his back on her for good. Shame lay, heavy and painful on his heart.

'I was so angry. So humiliated, Idris. I could have walked away. But he is my husband and you are my son and so I swallowed my pride and I stayed—although he knows there must be no more *affaires*. He may be French and an artist but I cannot abide anything as boring as a cliché. I know you don't see it, think it, but I love you, *yaa bunaaya*. I am so proud of you. But I just want you to be happy.'

'You don't think I am happy?'

'I know you're not. I think you're scared to be, Idris. I think you see your worth in work and solving problems and taking on the world. You were embarrassed by me, I know that. And I think that photo has embarrassed you too. Love is about forgiving, Idris. About looking beyond the obvious to what is real and true. About never being too proud to say sorry. And true happiness is loving and being loved, no matter how inconvenient, and I think you are too scared. And that must be on me. And I am so sorry.' Her large eyes shimmered with tears. Idris sat rigid and then sighed, leaning against her for the first time in a long, long time as her words sank in, each one painful in its truth.

'Thank you, *Maman*. I need to get back to London. Do you want to come with me and meet your grandson and your daughter-in-law? If she still wants to stay married to me, that is.'

CHAPTER THIRTEEN

NEITHER IDRIS NOR his mother spoke much on the walk back to the chateau, his mother's words spinning round and round in his head. She had never been the kind of mother to dish out advice or talk about feelings; he loved her, but, he acknowledged, maybe he'd allowed his view of her to be shaped by his disapproving grandparents, by the persona she adopted. He'd never wondered what it must be like being exiled from your home, cut off from your family, married to someone whose work always came before anyone and everything.

Shame flushed through him, scalding in its intensity. His mother had been badly hurt by his father's affair, so hurt she had turned to her only son for advice and help—and all Idris had wanted was to end the phone call and get back to work. Just as he had wanted to put Saskia in a taxi and close the door on her. He had thought his work, his peace more important than two people who had so desperately needed him. What kind of man did that make him?

And here he was doing the same again. Saskia had worked incredibly hard to fit in at the palace, to be the Queen Dalmaya needed her to be. She sat up late revising customs and history and language. She knew the names of the wives and children of everyone they met, when to speak and when to stand back. She had a gift of summing up a situation with one glance and defusing it or working out a solution, whether it was an air ambulance for the Al Bedi or a new community centre in the poverty-stricken town they had visited last. The only thing she complained about was not having enough to do.

How had he thanked her? By treating one mishap as a catastrophe. By freezing her out. Just as he'd frozen out his own mother. His fear of drama and confrontation when it came to anything personal meant he would rather walk away than sort out a difficult situation. Rather leave Saskia to face the press alone.

He loved both his grandfathers and was grateful for everything they had given him, but from them he had inherited a sense of shame. Shame every time his mother was on the front page of a gossip magazine, shame when his father's latest, controversial exhibition hit the headlines, shame when their relationship was the subject of speculation. From them he had learned the value of hard work, a good lesson it was true, but not of compassion. Of pride but not of humility.

Saskia knew all about humility and hard work. She was filled with more compassion than anyone he had ever known. She was straight and true, always putting her own needs last—which was why she needed him. Needed him to put her first. But he had let her down again.

There would be no third time. That he swore.

'I've messed everything up, *Maman*.' Idris felt her falter as he said the words, then she slipped an arm through his and squeezed it.

'Idris, you of all people know that there is nothing that can't be fixed. Just look at this place. Your grandfather left a tumbling-down building, cellars full of antique equipment and a work ethos steeped in traditions that were out of date before he was even born. In just a few years you have restored the chateau and made Delacour wine one of the most sought-after brands.'

'Places and things and figures I can fix, but neither Oxford nor the Sorbonne offered me a course in human emotions,' he said. 'Even if they had I probably wouldn't have taken it.'

'Do you love her? This Saskia?'

He winced at the directness in his mother's gaze. 'That's a complicated question.'

'No, no, *yaa bunaaya*. It's the easiest question of all. If the answer is no then you must decide whether you can live with a lifetime of duty with no chance of love. If the answer is yes then you must win her back.' She patted his arm. 'Don't worry. I'll help you.'

Idris touched his mother's hand in thanks while her question repeated over and over in his mind, in his heart. Did he love Saskia? He'd told her once that he'd been as close to loving her as a man like him could ever be. Was that true or was it a way of hiding from anything as messy and real as love?

He desired her, that was true enough. He respected her intelligence and compassion. He liked the soft expression that stole over her face when she was rocking Sami, as if he was the most precious thing in the world. He admired the way she had raised Jack, the comradeship between them, her determination to give him the best childhood she could. She frustrated him, her obstinacy out in the desert when she wouldn't allow him to call the helicopter—but it had paid off. The Al Bedi had been impressed by her courage and her insistence on owning the horse that had thrown her.

She was beautiful, that went without saying. But hers was a beauty that went beyond the physical, a sweetness in her soul that hadn't been soured by the hardships she'd endured.

And he desired her. No matter he had already listed it. It was important enough to list twice. He couldn't imagine holding another woman, kissing another woman. Loving another woman…

His hands curled into fists. Of course he loved her. How could he not? Deserve her? That was a different matter. He had to prove he deserved her, prove he was worthy, show her how much he loved her—everything that she was. He stepped up his pace, heading towards the chateau.

How did a man prove his love? Especially a man who had screwed up so royally. His brain began to tick, pulling in ideas and thoughts and images, discarding others. He'd always been a good problem solver, now was the time to prove it. 'Don't worry, *Maman*, I have a plan.' He fished his phone out of his pocket and searched for a number. 'Faye? Is Jack there? Great, pass him to me. I need to check something with him.' For his plan to work he needed to enlist some help and Jack was his go-to guy.

Saskia didn't know whether she was more grateful that Idris made it to London in the nick of time or furious that he had waited until barely a half hour before the social worker was due before sauntering in, a glamorous, petite woman at his side. It took her one glance to identify the woman as Zara Al Osman Delacour, the famous Runaway Princess herself. She didn't look scandalous in her neat little black suit, her coiled dark hair only lightly streaked with grey and an emotional smile on her face; she looked happy.

'Saskia, I am so excited to meet you at last. And you, Jack. I am to be your *grandmère*, I understand.' She pronounced the French word with a distinctly Anglo-Dalmayan accent. 'I have many, many plans for the two of us. I do hope you like trips out to exciting places. And this? This must be Sami.' Her face softened.

Saskia glanced over at Idris, uncomfortable with misleading his mother about Sami's parentage, but his expression was inscrutable and she couldn't catch his eye.

'Ah, he does look like Fayaz. That makes me so happy. A fragment of happiness from such a tragedy. Yes, Idris told me,' she said quietly as Saskia looked at her in surprise. 'You are a very brave young woman.'

'Thank you.' Saskia swallowed, the lump in her throat almost more than she could bear as Sami's great-aunt kissed him, sadness mingling with love on her vivid face.

'Fayaz came to visit me when he started Oxford,' Princess Zara said. 'He and Maya, he wanted to meet the fun side of his family, he told me. He was a lovely boy. I cherished my friendship with them. Thank you for giving them this hope, Saskia. And thank you for doing what needed to be done. It can't have been easy.'

'Nothing worth doing usually is,' Saskia replied, taking her son back, conscious of the older woman's scrutiny as she did so. She caught Idris's eye and for a moment she thought he was going to say something to her, but at that moment the social worker was announced and everything around her, every other emotion and problem, disappeared, her entire focus and will centred on convincing this stranger that she was a fit mother for the small boy.

Thankfully a scandal involving two reality-show stars, a fight and an arrest had lured the press away late last night so they could welcome the adoption official through the front door of the Embassy. She didn't mention the photo at all; the only hint that Saskia and Idris weren't like any normal couple looking to adopt came in a few questions about living with security and how Jack was adjusting to palace life. Luckily Jack was so enthusiastic about his life in Dalmaya the subject was quickly dropped.

'That's a lovely wee boy you have there,' the social worker said with a smile as Saskia saw her out at the end of the two-hour session. 'You've done a good job, Your Highness.'

'I've been very lucky,' Saskia answered, more than a little choked. 'What happens next?'

'Next?' The social worker looked surprised at the question. 'We'll notify your lawyers of the court date. I don't think you will be waiting long, not in a case as straightforward as this.'

Saskia waited until she had left before sagging against the wall. Straightforward? That had to be good, right? She glanced up the stairs to where the family were waiting for her. Idris had been wonderful throughout the interview, calm and measured, even when the questioning had felt intrusive, no hint of the coldness that had characterised the last week. And he had brought his mother to the Embassy—officially Dalmayan soil. The first time the Princess had been anywhere near her home country in over thirty years. Saskia didn't know what to think. All she knew was that it was time she and Idris had a good, long talk and this time she was going to be the one calling the shots.

Intentions were all very well, but try as she might

Saskia didn't manage to get Idris alone at any point for the rest of the morning. He disappeared several times for long periods, once or twice with Jack. If the idea didn't seem ridiculous, she would have said he was avoiding her on purpose. He didn't seem cold or angry—at times his expression rested on her with a heat that made her quiver. But every time she made a move to draw him away he slipped away so seamlessly she couldn't see how he had managed it.

'We need to talk,' she managed to quietly say as they finished a celebratory lunch in honour of Jack's interview and Idris paused, his gaze serious.

'I know. Later. I promise.'

Frustrated, she made to turn away and he caught her arm gently, pulling her around to face his scrutiny. 'You look tired.'

'I've not been sleeping, worrying about this interview I suppose. My head is pounding,' she admitted, softened by his concern.

'Why don't you lie down for a couple of hours? I'm sure two nannies, one man and one doting grandmother can take care of two boys for an afternoon.'

Excuses sprang to her lips. She didn't want to show weakness to anyone, especially not Idris, but the words wouldn't come. Truth was she was exhausted, physically and emotionally, and although an afternoon nap wouldn't cure either it could only help. 'Okay. I will. Thank you.'

The short sleep refreshed her more than she thought possible; a quick shower and a change of clothes and she felt like a new woman, ready to talk to Idris, ready to make sure her feelings were not just heard but that some kind of consensus about the future would be made. She put a hand to her stomach, trying to press away the nerves, the fear she might get this wrong. The boys deserved a loving family, that wasn't in doubt, she just needed to ensure there was a place for her in Idris's life. A place where she would be happy and respected if not loved.

The spacious living area seemed strangely quiet. Saskia wandered through the snug, the living room and the less formal sitting room used primarily by the boys, but there was no sign of anyone. She sat by the window and looked out at Kensington Gardens, feeling a little ridiculous at how forlorn she was. Of course there was a reasonable explanation for their absence; they were probably in the park. She was overtired and a little overwrought, that was all.

She blinked back a tear. 'I don't even know why I'm crying,' she said aloud. Maybe it was the relief that the adoption seemed to be going well. Maybe the anticlimax that after gearing herself up to tell Idris how she felt, she hadn't managed to say more than a few words to him. He couldn't just waltz in here and expect everything to be okay…

She should head out to the park and see if she could find them. Now the press had gone she'd be able to walk out of the front door and straight over the road like any normal tourist. Mind made up, Saskia headed back to the pretty master bedroom she had chosen to occupy, only to come to an abrupt halt. A small bag she had never seen before sat on her bed, a note on the top. Her heart sped up to a panicked thrum. That hadn't been there a few minutes ago. Who had put it there? Was Idris sending her away? She stared at the note for a long moment then slowly walked towards it, picking it up gingerly as if it might come to life under her fingertips.

There's a car downstairs.
You're expected at the London Palatial Hotel spa.
There may be scones.
Enjoy.
I

Saskia read the note through and then through again, her heart slowing as she took in the words. An afternoon to herself in a spa was an unusually thoughtful gesture—or not that unusual, she thought, fingering the charm bracelet she rarely took off. She took a deep, steadying breath. Maybe it would be a good thing to have some time out before she tackled Idris.

The famous spa was as imposingly luxurious as Saskia had heard, although as Princess Saskia of Dalmaya she was accorded the kind of reverential welcome plain Saskia Harper with her maxed-out credit card and second-hand clothes would never have enjoyed. She pushed that thought away, determined to wring the most out of the hot stone massage, facial and manicure that had been booked for her.

By the time she was escorted to the personal hot tub with rose petals sprinkled in the water and candles lit on every conceivable surface she felt like a new woman and ready for the difficult conversation that lay ahead. It wasn't that she didn't appreciate this thoughtful gesture, but she recognised that through her entire childhood she'd been bought off with lavish gifts. Her questions had never been answered. She had never found out why she didn't meet her father's dates, why her mother had left her, where her father's money had come from. Not until it all came crashing down.

She needed knowledge and agency, not just gestures.

Before she knew it her time was up and a smiling assistant helped her into one of the luxurious silk robes, guiding her to a small dressing room. Saskia stopped at the threshold and stared. A beautiful, full-length dress in her favourite pale pink hung on the wall, its cap sleeves embellished with a silver thread, the same thread accenting the waist and the hem, tiny delicate crystals shimmering in the chiffon overskirt. Silver sandals and a matching clutch bag were carefully placed on a stool and a make-up artist stood by the dressing table, the tools of her trade spread out in front of her. 'Please take a seat, Your Highness,' she said. 'Would you like your hair up or down?'

'I…' Saskia looked over at the dress again. 'I don't actually know where I'm going.' What on earth was going on? Her pulse sped up; surely she wasn't heading straight to an official event? Not when she was still living down the last one?

'Half and half, I think, if we're going to use this tiara.' The stylist held up a delicate silver chain punctuated with crystals in every twist.

'Fine. Thanks.' Every item in this room was perfect, exactly what she would have picked for herself, from the rose-pink bra and knickers draped over the chair behind her to the tiara dangling from the stylist's fingers. Only she had no idea who had chosen them for her and where she would be going in them.

Saskia took a deep breath, willing her panicked pulse to calm. She'd spent the last seven years micromanaging every second. It was the only way she had managed to survive. She didn't know what Idris expected from this gesture but as far as she was concerned their talk had just moved from important to urgent, and once they had had that talk she'd know whether she could stay with him, or if the marriage he offered was too painful for her to bear.

CHAPTER FOURTEEN

IDRIS PACED UP and down the famous domed foyer, reflecting that with all the marble and archways it was a little like being back in his own palace. He should feel at home, but, despite the coolness of the autumn evening, his suit felt too warm, too constricted. He pulled at his bow tie, wishing he'd opted for Dalmayan formal dress rather than the restrictions of a tuxedo. He glanced at his watch. Saskia should be here by now. Had he done the right thing, springing this on her? What if she hated it? What if he had got it all wrong? Relying on the judgement of a nine-year-old boy and of his impulsive mother could be the biggest mistake of all.

No, not the biggest mistake. That had happened seven years ago. It was time to atone.

His heart thumped as the great doors finally swung open. Saskia stood poised at the entrance, eyes wide as she looked in at the well-lit hall. 'What on earth are we doing at the V&A?' She stepped inside but made no move to come any closer to him.

'It's your favourite place.'

'Yes. But…' She shook her head, the soft waves of her hair rippling as she did so. 'I don't understand.'

'I wanted you to know that I notice things, that I'm not quite as cold, as unfeeling as I appear. I wanted you to know that I know your favourite colour is pink even though fashion tells you not to wear it.'

She tilted her chin at that, one hand touching the ends of her vibrant hair. 'It's a stupid rule.'

'You look beautiful in pink,' he said softly. His mother had picked out her dress with her unerring eye for style. Saskia was like a goddess of light, the silk and chiffon draping every curve and falling in folds to the floor. Marlowe's immortal words came back to him, just as they had that day at the library all those years before. She could launch one thousand ships, ten thousand and he would be at the very lead, doing whatever it took to win his wife back.

'I know afternoon tea is your favourite meal. How were the scones at the spa, by the way?'

'Delicious.' Her face was still suspicious. 'Everyone else was on watercress soup. I thought I might be lynched, especially when I spread the butter on extra thick.'

'I know that you prefer white gold to rose gold and your jewellery less ostentatious than Dalmayan fashion.' The delicate tiara flashed, wound through her fiery hair, and the charm bracelet glinted on her wrist. 'And I know I owe you an explanation.'

She held up one elegant hand. 'Idris, why did you put those clauses in the wedding contract?'

He stilled. This wasn't what he had expected her to say. 'Clauses?'

'Yes. I asked one of the embassy staff to translate it for me. There were clauses in there that weren't in the version my lawyer read to me. Handwritten clauses, which were evidently added after I'd approved the draft.' She watched him carefully. 'In the version I read I was to have appropriate alimony for the boys if we divorced. Generous alimony, life-changing alimony but appropriate. In the version I read this week I have been given the villa outright, I am allowed to divorce you at any time with no contest, keep full custody of the boys, as long as I bring Sami to Dalmaya every summer, and I'm entitled to the kind of alimony people tear each other apart in divorce courts for. That's not just generous, Idris.' She swallowed. 'That's an invitation. An invitation to divorce.'

He had added those clauses the night after they slept together, knowing they had crossed a line they might not be able to retreat back to. Idris held her gaze. 'I forced you into marrying me. I wanted to make sure you had options, a genuine choice.'

'I didn't go into this marriage intending to end it as soon as it got hard. I'm not saying I thought we'd grow old together but neither was I planning to cash my chips in and waltz out as quickly as I entered. My word means something, Idris.'

'I know.'

'Was it about giving me a choice or about giving me a push? I know I embarrassed you, embarrassed the palace…'

'No, Saskia. You didn't.' Here it was. The moment he had been both anxious for and dreading. The moment he told her who he was and what he was and allowed her to judge him. To walk away if he was unworthy. The moment Idris Delacour stopped hiding from life, from love, from the agony of feeling. 'The truth was I was jealous.'

'Jealous?'

'Jealous. You were having so much fun, and not with me. That's understandable.' He huffed out a laugh. 'I sent you into that room with a list of strictures and rules and didn't think for a moment that a woman in her twenties, a woman who's done nothing but be responsible for the last seven years, might need to unwind sometimes. Just because I never allow myself to unwind. When you fell I could have, should have laughed it off. It was nothing, but all I could see was headlines, judgements.'

He paused, searching for the right words to confess. 'The truth is I was still reeling from seeing how happy you had looked just before you fell, how happy you were away from the palace and the responsibilities I had forced on you. Those aren't escape clauses, Saskia, they are a promise that you can walk away any time. That I was wrong to bully you into this world. God knows, it's hard enough for me, and I at least had some training, some awareness of what it entails.'

Saskia's eyes were fixed on him, her gaze almost painful in its intensity. 'It was just so nice to see Robbie I forgot why I was there. What I should have done was arrange to see him later, at the palace, when you were there and we could have caught up away from prying eyes and cameras. I know that now. I was just so tired of everyone watching me, of being on display all the time, I relaxed too much. The fall was an accident but it wouldn't have happened if I'd been more careful.'

She took a deep breath. 'The thing is I can't guarantee I won't mess up again, Idris. In fact I can guarantee I will. I'm not trained for this, any of it, and I'm not naturally dignified like you and Maya. And that would be okay, if I thought you were on my side. But if you are going to freeze me out every time I mess up…' She shook her head. 'I don't need obscene alimony or want it. But if you're not on my side then I can't stay with you. Not even for the boys because they shouldn't have to grow up seeing that…'

His heart swelling, Idris walked over to his wife, to the woman he knew he loved so much he would let her walk away if that was what she needed—the woman he would then spend every moment winning back, proving he could love her the way she needed to be loved, valued for everything she was. He took her hands. 'Look at me, Saskia.'

She raised her eyes to his, the vulnerability in their depths striking him harder than anger or hatred ever could have.

'I am on your side,' he said. 'Always. It took me a while to realise that, but I am. I let you down, back when we were younger, and I let you down last week. I let you down because I put my pride first, because I didn't want to admit I was jealous. Because I didn't want to admit I loved you.'

The words echoed round and round the great hallway. 'You…you what?' Saskia was trembling, with hope, with the first glimmers of happiness, with fear that this was all a dream.

Idris's grip tightened on hers and she returned the pressure, holding on as if he were all that was holding her up. 'I love you, Saskia Harper. You have grown into an extraordinary, intelligent, compassionate woman and Dalmaya is lucky to have you as its Queen. Saskia, I am so proud to be able to call you my wife and I'm so sorry that I haven't made that clear, that, rather than show the world how much I love you, our wedding was behind closed doors.' He looked down at her, the dark eyes simmering. 'I said I wanted to give you choices, Saskia, and I am. Here, today.' His mouth quirked into a half-smile. 'If that's what you want, that is.'

'Choices?' All she could do was parrot the words back to him.

'Choices. And this time the choice is genuinely yours. Either we stay as we are, a marriage of convenience. Joint monarchs, parents, hopefully friends. I know it won't be easy, not after the events of the last few weeks, but I promise to work harder, to make it easier.'

Saskia could feel the beat of her heart, each one just that little bit faster than the one before, the rush of her blood around her shaking body. Could she go back to the marriage of convenience she had agreed to? Knowing that she loved him and that he loved her?

'Or,' he continued, 'you take advantage of the clauses in that contract and walk away, no hard feelings.'

Just like that she could have her life back. The house, the degree, the career. They didn't hold the allure they once had. She was beginning to love Dalmaya, the people and the desert and the all-encompassing heat. She could see a role there, a way to make her mark on the evolving country. 'They're my choices?' The hope had fizzled out, flat like left-out lemonade. He'd said he loved her but there was no love in this sterile pair of choices. She tried to tug her hands away but he still held them firmly in his grasp.

'No. There's one more.' The tenderness in his eyes was new and as Saskia stared into their dark depths she knew she had no defences against it. All she could do was stand there, holding onto him. 'Through there, in one of the galleries and the gardens, are your friends. Work colleagues who miss you, fellow students who can't wait to discuss essays with you, neighbours hoping you're coming back. Some of our old Oxford friends—including Rob—who mourn Maya and Fayaz as much as we do. Jack's old school friends and their parents.

You told me you had no one, Saskia, but when my mother, Faye, Lucy and I rang around the names Jack gave us I realised you made an impact on every person you knew. The mother whose sons you took to the park with Jack when her baby was colicky. The neighbour you made stews for when she was ill. The students you coached online. The other temps you supported through job after job. They all love you and they are all here.'

The litany of names was a revelation. Saskia felt the truth of Idris's words as each one sank in, warming her from within. She'd been too scared to let anyone in, to confide in them, to admit how hard it was but she hadn't been a lone wolf, not all the time.

'They're here?'

'Officially they've been invited to celebrate our new family, a party for Sami and Jack. But there's an official standing by ready to marry us, if that's what you want. If you want more than signing a contract in a language you don't understand. If you want to make vows, a commitment. Because that's what I want, Saskia, to tell the world how much I love and cherish you. To make you my wife in more than name, to make you the wife of my heart.'

It took several moments for his words to register. To realise just what he was saying. 'I...I...' She pulled her hands away and placed them on her hips. 'You call that a proposal, Your Highness Sheikh Idris Delacour Al Osman?'

The anxiety vanished from his eyes as Idris's mouth tilted into his rare and, oh, so sweet smile. 'Sheikha Saskia Harper, Princess, mother, wife, Queen. Will you do me the very great honour of becoming my wife in reality as well as in name?' He reached into his pocket and pulled out a box, opening it up as he sank onto one knee before her. 'Rubies, Saskia. Red like your hair, like the desert sunset, like the fire in my soul. A fire I didn't even know existed until I met you.'

At his words her heart swelled, all the love she had been keeping banked up, hidden away, finally rushing free, filling every nerve, every atom, every cell with the knowledge she was his as he was hers. Saskia stared at the antique ring, her heart swelling, then back at Idris, allowing herself to soak in the tenderness, the hope and passion in his eyes.

'Yes. Of course I will. I thought I loved you when I was nineteen, and in some ways I did, but I was just a child. I didn't really understand what love was. But I do love you now, with all my heart, and I want to marry you, properly, with vows and meaning and love. Yes, I do.'

Idris slid the delicate ring carefully onto her finger before getting up, joy writ all over his usually impassive face. 'You won't regret it,' he vowed as he held her close. 'I love you, Saskia.'

Looking up at him, she saw the truth of it and knew that although their road would never be an easy one if they could walk it together they could face anything.

* * * * *

If you enjoyed this story, check out these other great reads from Jessica Gilmore:

A PROPOSAL FROM THE CROWN PRINCE
HER NEW YEAR BABY SECRET
UNVEILING THE BRIDESMAID
IN THE BOSS'S CASTLE

All available now!

Hardback – October 2017

ROMANCE

Claimed for the Leonelli Legacy	Lynne Graham
The Italian's Pregnant Prisoner	Maisey Yates
Buying His Bride of Convenience	Michelle Smart
The Tycoon's Marriage Deal	Melanie Milburne
Undone by the Billionaire Duke	Caitlin Crews
His Majesty's Temporary Bride	Annie West
Bound by the Millionaire's Ring	Dani Collins
The Virgin's Shock Baby	Heidi Rice
Whisked Away by Her Sicilian Boss	Rebecca Winters
The Sheikh's Pregnant Bride	Jessica Gilmore
A Proposal from the Italian Count	Lucy Gordon
Claiming His Secret Royal Heir	Nina Milne
Sleigh Ride with the Single Dad	Alison Roberts
A Firefighter in Her Stocking	Janice Lynn
A Christmas Miracle	Amy Andrews
Reunited with Her Surgeon Prince	Marion Lennox
Falling for Her Fake Fiancé	Sue MacKay
The Family She's Longed For	Lucy Clark
Billionaire Boss, Holiday Baby	Janice Maynard
Billionaire's Baby Bind	Katherine Garbera

0917 GEN STD HB

MILLS & BOON®

Large Print – October 2017

ROMANCE

Sold for the Greek's Heir	Lynne Graham
The Prince's Captive Virgin	Maisey Yates
The Secret Sanchez Heir	Cathy Williams
The Prince's Nine-Month Scandal	Caitlin Crews
Her Sinful Secret	Jane Porter
The Drakon Baby Bargain	Tara Pammi
Xenakis's Convenient Bride	Dani Collins
Her Pregnancy Bombshell	Liz Fielding
Married for His Secret Heir	Jennifer Faye
Behind the Billionaire's Guarded Heart	Leah Ashton
A Marriage Worth Saving	Therese Beharrie

HISTORICAL

The Debutante's Daring Proposal	Annie Burrows
The Convenient Felstone Marriage	Jenni Fletcher
An Unexpected Countess	Laurie Benson
Claiming His Highland Bride	Terri Brisbin
Marrying the Rebellious Miss	Bronwyn Scott

MEDICAL

Their One Night Baby	Carol Marinelli
Forbidden to the Playboy Surgeon	Fiona Lowe
A Mother to Make a Family	Emily Forbes
The Nurse's Baby Secret	Janice Lynn
The Boss Who Stole Her Heart	Jennifer Taylor
Reunited by Their Pregnancy Surprise	Louisa Heaton

MILLS & BOON®

Hardback – November 2017

ROMANCE

The Italian's Christmas Secret	Sharon Kendrick
A Diamond for the Sheikh's Mistress	Abby Green
The Sultan Demands His Heir	Maya Blake
Claiming His Scandalous Love-Child	Julia James
Valdez's Bartered Bride	Rachael Thomas
The Greek's Forbidden Princess	Annie West
Kidnapped for the Tycoon's Baby	Louise Fuller
A Night, A Consequence, A Vow	Angela Bissell
Christmas with Her Millionaire Boss	Barbara Wallace
Snowbound with an Heiress	Jennifer Faye
Newborn Under the Christmas Tree	Sophie Pembroke
His Mistletoe Proposal	Christy McKellen
The Spanish Duke's Holiday Proposal	Robin Gianna
The Rescue Doc's Christmas Miracle	Amalie Berlin
Christmas with Her Daredevil Doc	Kate Hardy
Their Pregnancy Gift	Kate Hardy
A Family Made at Christmas	Scarlet Wilson
Their Mistletoe Baby	Karin Baine
The Texan Takes a Wife	Charlene Sands
Twins for the Billionaire	Sarah M. Anderson

1017 GEN STD HB

MILLS & BOON®

Large Print – November 2017

ROMANCE

The Pregnant Kavakos Bride	Sharon Kendrick
The Billionaire's Secret Princess	Caitlin Crews
Sicilian's Baby of Shame	Carol Marinelli
The Secret Kept from the Greek	Susan Stephens
A Ring to Secure His Crown	Kim Lawrence
Wedding Night with Her Enemy	Melanie Milburne
Salazar's One-Night Heir	Jennifer Hayward
The Mysterious Italian Houseguest	Scarlet Wilson
Bound to Her Greek Billionaire	Rebecca Winters
Their Baby Surprise	Katrina Cudmore
The Marriage of Inconvenience	Nina Singh

HISTORICAL

Ruined by the Reckless Viscount	Sophia James
Cinderella and the Duke	Janice Preston
A Warriner to Rescue Her	Virginia Heath
Forbidden Night with the Warrior	Michelle Willingham
The Foundling Bride	Helen Dickson

MEDICAL

Mummy, Nurse...Duchess?	Kate Hardy
Falling for the Foster Mum	Karin Baine
The Doctor and the Princess	Scarlet Wilson
Miracle for the Neurosurgeon	Lynne Marshall
English Rose for the Sicilian Doc	Annie Claydon
Engaged to the Doctor Sheikh	Meredith Webber